Rudeus

jerd

Eris

DRAMATIS
PERSONAE

"That aside, state your name!"

"Rudeus Greyrat."

"Very good! I am Kishirika Kishirisu! People call me the...

Great Emperor of the Demon World!"

Kishirika

Roxy

Geese

Mushoku Tensei

jobless reincarnation

WRITTEN BY
Rifujin na Magonote

ILLUSTRATED BY
Shirotaka

Seven Seas Entertainment

MUSHOKU TENSEI
~ISEKAI ITTARA HONKI DASU~ VOL. 4

© Rifujin na Magonote 2014
Illustrations by Shirotaka

First published in Japan in 2014 by
KADOKAWA CORPORATION, Tokyo.
English translation rights arranged with
KADOKAWA CORPORATION, Tokyo.

Seven Seas press and purchase enquiries can be sent to
Marketing Manager Lianne Sentar at press@gomanga.com.
Information requiring the distribution and purchase of
digital editions is available from Digital Manager CK Russell
at digital@gomanga.com.

Follow Seven Seas Entertainment online at
sevenseasentertainment.com.

TRANSLATION: Alyssa Orton-Niioka
ADAPTATION: JY Yang
COVER DESIGN: KC Fabellon
INTERIOR LAYOUT & DESIGN: Clay Gardner
PROOFREADER: Dayna Abel, Stephanie Cohen
LIGHT NOVEL EDITOR: Nibedita Sen
MANAGING EDITOR: Julie Davis
EDITOR-IN-CHIEF: Adam Arnold
PUBLISHER: Jason DeAngelis

ISBN: 978-1-64505-179-4
Printed in Canada
First Printing: January 2020
10 9 8 7 6 5 4 3 2 1

Contents

CHAPTER 1:	Wind Port	11
CHAPTER 2:	Missed Connections, the Prequel	37
CHAPTER 3:	Missed Connections, the Sequel	61
SIDE STORY:	Missed Connections, Extra Story	95
CHAPTER 4:	The Sage on Board	123
CHAPTER 5:	The Demon in the Warehouse	145
CHAPTER 6:	The Beastfolk Children	163
CHAPTER 7:	Free Apartment	189
CHAPTER 8:	Fire Emergency	213
CHAPTER 9:	Slow Life in the Doldia Village	247
CHAPTER 10:	The Holy Sword Highway	277
EXTRA CHAPTER:	Guardian Fitz	307

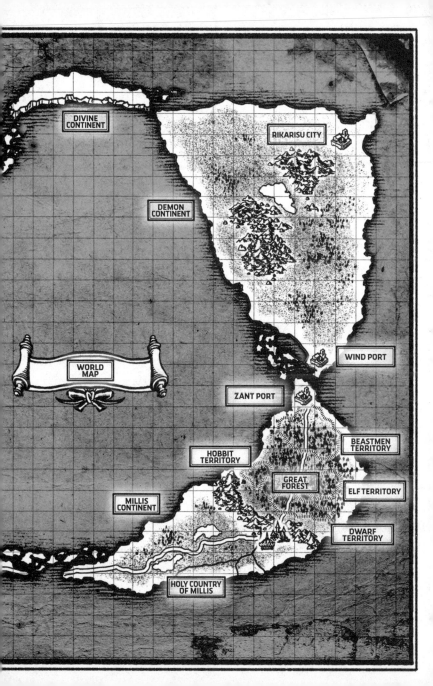

"It's nice when everyone is different. But it's even better when we're the same."

AUTHOR: RUDEUS GREYRAT
TRANSLATION: JEAN RF MAGOTT

CHAPTER 1
Wind Port

MY NAME IS Rudeus Greyrat, and I'm a pretty boy who just celebrated my eleventh birthday a few days ago. As a skilled magician, I've gained notoriety for my ability to use magic without chanting spells and my unique way of mixing the different elements.

One year ago, I was caught in a magical disaster and teleported to the Demon Continent. My hometown was on the exact opposite side of the map in the Asura Kingdom's Fittoa Region, which meant I had to travel halfway across the world to get back.

I became an adventurer to earn money as I started out on the long voyage home. In the past year, I've successfully cut my way across the Demon Continent.

Wind Port, the Demon Continent's one and only port city, was a townscape with rolling hills. From the entrance, you had a sweeping view of the entire city. Most of the houses were made with mud and stone in the Continent's typical style, but there was the occasional wooden house here and there. At the edge of the city was the harbor. That, rather than the main entrance, was where most of the hubbub took place and the peddlers set up shop.

It was a city with a flavor uniquely its own, different from the others I had seen before. Beyond the harbor, across from the city, the sea spread out vast and wide. When was the last time I had seen the ocean? Probably back when I attended a middle school on the coast.

This world was different from ours, but the sea was not. It was the same blue, had the same sound of crashing waves, and birds that looked just like seagulls. There were even sailboats. It was the first time I'd ever set my eyes on one. I saw them occasionally in movies, but seeing the real thing—made of wood with its cloth sails unfurled, gliding through the water—made my heart pound as if I were still a young boy.

There must be some mechanism in this world that allowed a boat to sail against a headwind. Actually, considering the world I was in, maybe they propelled themselves forward using wind magic.

"Look!"

The moment we arrived in the city, the red-haired girl riding the lizard with me suddenly leaped up. Her name was Eris Boreas Greyrat. She was the granddaughter of Sauros, the Liege Lord of Asura Kingdom's Fittoa Region, and also my pupil back when I worked as a tutor for their house. She was ferocious and spoiled rotten when we first met, but she'd become more flexible recently—enough to listen to what people had to say. She had been teleported together with me, and I had to see her safely back home.

"Look, Rudeus! The ocean!" The words that passed her lips were in fluent Demon God tongue. I had stressed the importance of speaking it all the time; Ruijerd and I also spoke in Demon God tongue as much as possible. As a result, Eris' language abilities had increased dramatically as of late. It was as I suspected: The quickest way to improve in a foreign language was to use it as often as possible. Granted, Eris couldn't read or write in the language at all. It wasn't that difficult a language, but it also wasn't something that could be mastered in a year.

On the other hand, I hadn't taught her any magic since coming to the Demon Continent. So not only could she not cast spells without chanting, but she had probably also forgotten the chants themselves.

"Eris, wait! Where are you going? We haven't even figured out where we're staying for the night!"

Eris stopped in her tracks when I called after her. This was the third time we'd had this exchange since we came to the Demon Continent. The first time, she got lost; the second, she got into a fight on a street corner. I wasn't going to have a third incident.

"Oh yeah! I'll get lost again if we don't decide on an inn first!" She bounded back to us, constantly glancing over her shoulder at the sea.

Come to think of it, this was probably the first time she'd seen something like this. There were some rivers near Fittoa, and apparently Sauros took her there on his days off and let her play in the water. Sadly, I never went with them, so I had no idea how much she knew about bodies of water.

"Can we swim?"

I tilted my head at her words. "You want to swim in the harbor?"

"I do!"

I might have wanted this for selfish reasons, but it was a wish destined to be unfulfilled. Namely because an important component was missing from this equation.

"You don't have a swimsuit, do you?" I asked.

"What the heck is a swimsuit? I don't need one!"

Her response was so shocking I couldn't hide my con-fusion. *What the heck is a swimsuit, I don't need one*, she said. So she meant to swim totally naked...? No, no way, that couldn't be it. Most likely she meant to swim in her underwear. I pictured her clad in nothing but her under-wear, water pouring over her. The damp fabric would cling to her body, and through the sheer material I would be able to see the color of her skin, as well as the slight protrusions on her chest.

Why didn't I ever join them when she went to play in the water back in Fittoa? Oh yes, because I was busy. Even on my days off I was preoccupied with something. Still, I should have gone with her just one time at least.

No, now wasn't the time to think about that. I needed to focus on the city right before me. Live in the now. That's right, live in the now! Woo-hoo, the ocean!

"No, you shouldn't swim in this ocean." A voice cut in from behind like a bucket of ice-cold water.

When I looked back, Ruijerd was sitting there with his bald head and a scar stretched across his face, like a yakuza. His full name was Ruijerd Superdia. He was a demon, one who loved children and had taken it upon himself to escort us from the very beginning, when we were so lost we didn't know up from down. Now that he was bald, it was impossible to tell that he had the infamous emerald-green hair of the Superd race. In this world, demons with emerald green hair were regarded as a symbol of fear. Ruijerd had cut his hair off for our sake. Restoring honor to the name of his people was just one way I could repay my debt to him.

"There's a lot of monsters in there."

A red jewel embedded in Ruijerd's forehead provided him with a sixth sense. It acted as a radar that could detect the presence of every living creature within several hundred meters of its bearer. With such a convenient ability, it was easy to think we could swiftly dispatch all those creatures in the ocean, but maybe it wasn't as all-powerful as I thought. Maybe those murky depths were impenetrable.

Nah. Even so, we should still be able to swim for a little bit, right? Swimming in the harbor might be too dangerous, but I could at least use earth magic on a nearby beach to make our own little pool.

No...there was still a chance it could be dangerous. There were beasts out there with powers of their own. Some of them might be able to jump over my barrier. It might be a sexy encounter if it were an octopus, but if it were a shark, we'd be in a real-life reenactment of *Jaws*.

There was little choice. Probably best to give up the idea of a swim in the ocean. There really was nothing else we could do. "There'll be no sea bathing this time. Let's go find our inn and then hit up the Adventurers' Guild."

"Okay..." Eris looked dejected.

Hmm. I was still very much interested in seeing how toned her body was. We hadn't much opportunity to check out each other's growth in the last year. It was difficult to gauge anything through her clothes, but maybe if we were out on the open beach, I could see a little more. *Yeah, that's right, we should do that.*

"Even if we can't go in the water, we could at least play on the beach, right?"

"The beach?"

"There's something called sand by the ocean. At the water's edge, that sand stretches out pretty far," I explained.

"And what part of that is supposed to be fun?" Eris asked.

"On the beach, you can squirt water on yourself and..."

"Rudeus, you've got that weird look on your face again."

"Ugh." Apparently, my expressions changed too easily with my emotions.

As I tried to clean the lecherous look off my face, Eris turned her eyes to the ocean and smiled. "But it sounds interesting! Let's do that afterward!" She happily kicked off and soared through the air, returning to the lizard. It was an incredible leap. Just the sound of her takeoff made me jump—it was like a low thumping noise. She had really toned her legs and lower body. Right now that really complemented her build, but I imagine her becoming even more brawny and muscular in the future, and that worried me a little.

Once we decided on our inn and boarded our lizard, we headed straight for the Adventurers' Guild. A diverse crowd of adventurers clamored around the Wind Port Adventurers' Guild. It wasn't an unfamiliar sight, but it seemed there were a considerable number of humans present this time. Once I crossed over to the Millis Continent, their numbers would surely increase exponentially.

There was an uncertain look on Ruijerd's face as I went to check out the bulletin board as I always did. "I thought we were going to cross the sea immediately?"

"I'm just looking. I heard that you can make a better income on the Millis Continent, anyway."

You could make a better income on the Millis Continent because the currency was different. The Millis Continent currency was broken up into six types: the king dollar, the general dollar, gold coins, silver coins, large copper coins, and copper coins. Comparing this to the Demon Continent's cheapest currency, which was the stone coin:

$$
\begin{aligned}
\text{1 king's dollar} &= \text{50,000 stone coins} \\
\text{1 general's dollar} &= \text{10,000 stone coins} \\
\text{1 gold coin} &= \text{5,000 stone coins} \\
\text{1 silver coin} &= \text{1,000 stone coins} \\
\text{1 large copper coin} &= \text{100 stone coins} \\
\text{1 small copper coin} &= \text{10 stone coins}
\end{aligned}
$$

A B-ranked mission in the Demon Continent netted you about five to ten scrap iron coins. That converted into 150-200 stone coins. If Millis Continent's B-ranked missions were worth—let's assume—five large copper coins, that would be 1,500 stone coins. That was ten times as much. We were better off making money on Millis Continent.

That said, if we had time to kill before our ship was ready, then we would probably take one of the jobs here. Generally, that meant B-ranked missions. Not only were A-ranked and S-ranked missions dangerous, most of them took more than a week to complete. If we wanted a consistent daily income, then B-ranked jobs were our best option. It was also why I had no plan to raise our party to S-rank, because it would mean we could no longer accept B-ranked missions.

In fact, as an A-ranked party you could undertake S-ranked missions anyway, so I initially questioned the need for having an S-rank in the party ranking system at all. When I asked one of the guild personnel about it, they told me there were special benefits if you rose to S-rank. I didn't pry any further, but I guessed it meant getting bigger discounts for lodging, being allotted better-quality guild jobs, or the assurance that they would turn a blind eye to some of a party's illegal behavior. Something along those lines.

Those who benefited the most from those perks were primarily the adventurers who went dungeon-diving into labyrinths. Our party had no such plans. It was dangerous and it took days to finish such a venture. Our missions were primarily B-ranked, and we had no designs on moving up to S-rank any time soon.

Eris, of course, disagreed on that point.

Digressions aside, we were adventurers primarily interested in earning money, so if going to Millis Continent was the fastest way to do that, boarding a ship immediately was in our best interest.

"By the way, where do the boats leave from?" I asked.

"The harbor, of course."

"Yes, but *where* in the harbor?"

"Ask someone," Ruijerd said.

"Yes, sir."

I moved to the counter. Standing behind it was a human woman. In fact, most personnel tended to be women, and for some reason they tended to be generously endowed, probably for aesthetic purposes.

"I'd like to go to Millis Continent," I explained. "Do you know what I should do to get there?"

"Please direct those questions to the checkpoint."

"Checkpoint?"

"Once you board a boat, you'll be beyond our country's borders."

In other words, the guild had no jurisdiction over international travel, so its personnel had no responsibility to guide me in those matters. Hm. In that case, it was time to head toward the checkpoint. Then, just as I was about to ask for a more in-depth explanation...

"Hey, you!"

A loud voice echoed through the room. When I looked back, Eris had punched some male human. It seemed our nuclear warhead was feeling particularly explosive today.

"Just who and where do you think you were touching?!"

"I-It was an accident! Who the hell would want to touch an ass like yours, anyway?"

"I don't care if it was an accident or not! Your apology isn't!" Eris had grown quite proficient in the Demon tongue. The better she got, the more frequently she got into fights. It clearly wasn't such a good thing that she knew what the other party was saying after all.

"Gahahaha! What's this, a fight?!"

"Go on, get 'em!"

"Come on, don't let a kid kick your ass!"

Fights between guild members were such a common daily occurrence that the guild didn't even bother getting involved. In fact, some of the personnel even took part by placing bets.

"I'll crush you under my feet!"

"I-I'm sorry, I admit defeat. Please let me go, don't grab my leg, stooop!"

While I was distracted, Eris had thrown the man on the ground. Lately, she'd become an expert in backing a person into a wall. She would snap without warning and decimate her opponent with incredible precision. In the time I spent wondering what she could possibly be pissed about, she already had her foot pressed firmly into her opponent's weak spot. Those C-ranked adventurers were no match for her.

Whenever her quarrels reached a certain point, Ruijerd would always step in. "Stop," he said.

"Lay off, I'm not going to stop!"

"You already won," Ruijerd said. "Let it go."

The same spectacle as always. I couldn't really stop her. Mostly because my way of stopping her was throwing my arms around her from behind, at which point my life would be the one in danger.

Someone shouted, "A bald guy and a ferocious redheaded girl...! Could you guys be Dead End?"

Silence fell across the hall, and then:

"Dead End... You mean that demon from the Superd race...?"

"Idiot! The party name. Those fakes all the rumors have been about lately!"

"I've heard rumors about the real thing, too."

Oh?

"I heard they're brutal, but he's not a bad guy at heart."

"So he's brutal but he's nice? C'mon, that's a contradiction."

"No, I meant not all of them are brutal."

The guild fell into hushed murmurs.

This was the first time we had experienced something like this. Apparently, our group had become quite famous. I guess we didn't have to spread Ruijerd's good name here after all, huh?

"They're an A-ranked party with just three people, after all."

"Yeah, that's incredible. Real thing or not, that's gotta be them."

"Mad Dog Eris and Guard Dog Ruijerd, right?"

The two of them had nicknames! Mad Dog and Guard Dog, huh? I wondered why they were both dogs. Also, what kind of dog did that make me, then? I tried to picture this for a minute. Certainly not a fighting dog. I hadn't done anything grand enough to earn that title, and I didn't seem gallant at all, either. In the past year, I had acted as the leader for the group. So maybe a more intellectual name, like Faithful Dog.

"Then that little midget over there must be Kennel Master Ruijerd!"

"I heard the Kennel Master is the nastiest one of all."

"Yeah, all he's done is awful things."

What in the world!!

Not only was the nickname different than I'd imagined, they didn't even remember my name! No, wait, but it *was* true that I used Ruijerd's name all the time, right? Still, whenever I did anything good, I would always proclaim, "I'm Ruijerd of Dead End, and don't you forget it!" Meanwhile, every time I did something bad, I would cackle loudly and say, "My name is Rudeus, bwahahaha!" So they shouldn't have gotten the two mixed up, right?

Hmm. After a whole year of laborious work, it was a bit of shock to discover people remembered everyone's name but mine. Oh well. It seemed I had a negative image attached to me, but at least people weren't using my real name. Besides, Kennel Master wasn't such a bad title. I wonder what Eris would think of it?

"But he's pretty small."

"Bet he's small down there too, since he's a kid and all!"

"Hey, hey! You start calling it small and he'll set his dogs loose on you!"

"Gahahaha!"

Before I realized what was happening, they were all laughing at me over something completely unrelated. Too bad for them, though. I was still growing (and coming along nicely, at that), so yes, it might be little more than a bamboo shoot for now. But the day it would grow into a magnificent, robust tree wasn't far off.

Ah, forget that. If we kept getting laughed at like this, Eris would go back into demon rage mode...or so I thought. Instead, she kept stealing glances at me with her cheeks flushed bright red. Aww, how adorable.

"Eris, what's wrong?"

"I-It's nothing!"

Heh heh heh. If you're that interested, then why don't you take a look while I'm showering tonight? Don't worry,

I'll explain everything to Ruijerd. If you want, we can even get in together. Of course, a hand, leg, body, or even a tongue might slip in the process...

Anyway, enough joking around. It was time for us to move on to the checkpoint. I would leave here with every bit of dignity expected of a "Kennel Master."

"Miss Eris, Mister Ruijerdoria! Let's be on our way!"

"Why do you screw up my name like that...?"

"Hmph!"

We departed with the attention of most of the guild trained on the three of us.

We arrived at the checkpoint. This city was located in the Demon Continent, but the boat we wanted to board would take us to the Holy Country of Millis. If you were carrying any luggage, you would have to pay taxes, and entry into the country itself would cost money as well. This was either to prevent crime or simply an opportunity for profit. My curiosity aside, we would pay if they said we had to.

"How much would it cost for us? We have two humans and one demon in our party."

"Two humans would be five steel iron coins. Which demon tribe?"

"Superd."

The checkpoint official jerked their gaze toward Ruijerd with a start. When they realized he was bald, they let out a heavy sigh, like they were put upon by just addressing us. "It'll be two hundred green ore coins for the Superd."

"T-two hundred?!" Now it was my turn to be the one in shock. "Wh-why is it so high?!"

"I'm sure you already know the answer."

Of course I knew it! I had traveled with Ruijerd for the past year, how wouldn't I know? There was such contempt toward the Superd tribe that all its members were groundlessly persecuted. Even so, this fee was too high.

"But why such an impossibly high sum?"

"Don't ask me. Ask the person who decided on it."

I pressed on. "Well, why do *you* think it's so high?"

"Uh, well, to prevent terrorism, I'm sure, in case someone brings one along as a slave and sets them loose on the Millis Continent." At least, that was his interpretation. In other words, they were treating the Superd as if they were a ticking time bomb.

"You're those guys, Dead End, right? The fake Superd. When you board, they'll check what subrace you are. Don't act tough and waste two hundred green ore coins here when they'll figure you out anyway."

The official's words of caution were a blessing in disguise. This meant we wouldn't be able to pretend Ruijerd was from the Migurd tribe because we'd be discovered anyway.

"If you lie about your tribe, you don't have to pay a fine, do you?"

"Just the money you wasted by lying about it in the first place." In other words, as long as we paid the money like he told us, we would be fine. The power of money was impressive indeed.

The sun was already going down by the time we departed from the checkpoint. We decided to return to the inn and eat. We were provided with the port city's unique seafood cuisine. The main dish was the size of a fist, steamed in rice wine with a touch of garlic butter. It was delicious, easily the best thing I had eaten since we arrived on the Demon Continent.

"This is so good!" Eris said happily as she chewed, her cheeks stuffed with food.

In this past year she had entirely forgotten the Asura Kingdom's customary table manners. She cut her food with the knife in her right hand, then stabbed it and put it straight in her mouth. At least she wasn't shoveling it in with her fists, but there was nothing graceful or refined about it. Edna, her etiquette tutor, would surely be reduced to tears if she could see Eris now. This was also my responsibility.

"Eris, your table manners are awful!"

Munch, munch. "Who the hell's worried about manners?"

In comparison, Ruijerd's manners were much better, although they had no elegance to them, either. He didn't use his knife at all, but used his fork both to cut the food and eat. He slid his fork through the fish as easily as if it were butter. The skills of an expert, no doubt.

"Well, I realize we're still in the midst of our meal, but let's start our strategy meeting."

"Rudeus, talking during a meal is poor manners," Eris said, suddenly wearing the expression of a prim and proper lady on her face.

We started our meeting once the meal was over and our bellies were full.

"It's going to cost two hundred green ore for us to cross the sea. A ridiculous price."

"Sorry. It's because of me." Ruijerd's face clouded over.

Even I never imagined it would cost this much. Frankly, I'd completely underestimated the fee. I thought that making a little coin along the way would let us cross the ocean easily. In reality, it was five silver coins for humans. Even other demon tribes would pay one or two green ore coins at most. Only the fees for the Superd tribe were abnormally high.

"Now now, let's not say things like that, Pops."

"I'm not your father."

"I know," I said. "It was a joke."

That aside, two hundred coins was no ordinary amount of money. Even if we prioritized taking on S-ranked and A-ranked jobs, it would take us years to save up that much. It seemed the Millis Continent really didn't want any Superd crossing its borders.

"We're in a bind. We can't just leave Ruijerd behind."

Leaving Ruijerd behind would be the quickest way to make the crossing. The two of us were fairly experienced adventurers by now, so we could continue our journey even without him. That said, I had no intention of doing that. Ruijerd was going to be with us until our journey was over. Our friendship was unbreakable and eternal, after all. "Of course we won't leave him behind."

"Then what are we going to do?"

"We have...three options," I said, holding up the corresponding number of fingers. There were always three options for everything. One was to move forward, one was to go back, and the other was to stay where we were.

"Ah."

"Amazing, there's three whole options?" Eris asked.

"Heh heh!" I laughed.

Now just hold on, I thought. *I haven't thought through all of them yet. Let's see...*

"The first option is a frontal attack: we stay here, earn money, and travel to Millis Continent by paying the fee."

"But if we do that..."

"Yes, it will take way too much time," I agreed.

If we prioritized making money, we might be able to save the required sum within a year. However, there was no guarantee something wouldn't happen to it at some point, like us losing our coin purse.

"The second option: we go into a labyrinth and obtain a magic crystal or magic item. This would be a laborious task, but we might be able to get the money we need in a single mission." A magic crystal would net a high price. As for how much exactly, I couldn't say, but if we handed it over to the official at the checkpoint, he might even let a Superd through.

"A labyrinth! I like the sound of that! Let's do it!"

"No." Ruijerd shot down that plan immediately.

"Why not?!"

Ruijerd could easily detect living creatures with his sixth sense, but the traps within a labyrinth were probably a different matter.

"I really want to go," Eris said, pouting.

"It's an option, but one I'd rather not go with."

We might be fine if we proceeded with caution, but since I was rather careless with my feet, we would definitely make a fatal misstep at some point. It seemed prudent to heed Ruijerd's words on this one.

"The third option: we find a smuggler in this city who can take us."

"A smuggler? What the heck is that?"

"Where country borders are involved, you usually have to pay taxes to carry things across. That's why we were told to pay a fee. If you're a merchant, you most likely have to pay taxes on your goods, right?"

"I don't know, do you?"

"Yes, you do," I answered. Otherwise there would be no point in charging a greater fee based on a person's race. "And there are probably items that cost an insane amount in tax. So there should be someone here who does that job for a cheaper price, as well as handling illegal goods." Well, maybe there wasn't. But if there was, then we could surely have them take us across for a much lower price than two hundred green ore coins. There was clearly something going on with the fee at the checkpoint. That official told us we wouldn't be punished even if we lied about Ruijerd's tribe.

Anyway, I had just learned the hard way that the easiest path was the one riddled with traps. So while I included that as a potential option, I wanted to avoid doing anything unlawful if possible. For the moment, the three options that I had come up with were:

- The straightforward approach of earning money and paying the fee
- Making a killing by dungeon diving in a labyrinth
- Striking a deal with a smuggler

None of them were particularly good. Oh, right, there was one more. I could sell my staff, Aqua Heartia. It had an enormous magic crystal and was an Asura Kingdom masterwork. That would at least earn enough money for a member of the Superd race to cross the ocean.

Pros and cons aside, I didn't want to sell it if at all possible. It was a precious birthday gift from Eris, and I was making good use of it. Eris and Ruijerd surely wouldn't agree to me letting go of it so easily.

That night, a divine message came to me.

The Man-God told me, "Buy some food at a street stall and search the alleyways by yourself."

Sounds like a real pain in the ass. But since I have no other options, I'll try to be optimistic and give it a shot.

"So you're doing it because you have no other choice?"

Nah, I just already know what's going to happen since you said the words "food" and "back alleyway".

"Do you?"

Yeah, pretty cliché, right? Let me guess, I'm going to find some hungry kid that got lost. And she's going to have some weird guy trying to pick her up. How's that?

"You're exactly right. Incredible!"

Then that kid turns out to be the grandchild of the leader of the Shipwrights' Guild or something like that, right?

"Heh heh heh. Save the surprise for tomorrow."

What surprise? There hasn't been a single enjoyable surprise this entire time. Besides, dude! What the heck? It's been a whole year since you did this. I even thought I'd never have to see your face again!

"Ah, you see, last time my advice didn't turn out so well for you, did it? So it was a bit hard for me to show myself again."

Huh! So the Man-God has a little shame after all, I guess. But don't get the wrong idea, okay? That was my mistake the last time. That said, what was the correct choice I should have made?

"Well, if you want to use the term 'correct', that's on you. The 'normal' choice would have been to turn that lot into the guards, thereby solidifying your friendship with Ruijerd."

What? You're telling me the solution was that simple?

"That's right. I never dreamed you would make them your allies and earn the attention of those conniving small fries in the Adventurers' Guild. What an entertaining watch it was for me."

Yeah, and I didn't have the least bit of fun.

"But thanks to that, you managed to get this far in a year."

So you're saying the ends justify the means?

"Results mean everything."

Tch, I don't like that.

"You don't, eh? Well, that's up to you. Anyway, you seem to be in a foul mood, so I'll be off."

Wait just a second! There's one thing I want to confirm.

"And that is?"

If I don't think too hard about the advice you give me, does that mean things will go well?

"It's more entertaining for me if you give it a lot of thought."

Aha, so that's it! That's your game. Now I get it. Thanks for the tip. Next time it won't be so entertaining for you.

"Heh heh. I look forward to that, too."

Yeah, yeah, yeah. Of course you do.

My consciousness faded as those final words echoed in my head.

CHAPTER 2

Missed Connections, the Prequel

THE NEXT DAY, I went out and loaded my arms with food from one of the stalls before wandering the back alleys for a bit. The food was all roasted and skewered. There were some scallops similar to the ones we had in Japan, a fish similar to horse mackerel, and a few other sea creatures I couldn't identify. The stall owner didn't clarify what his wares were, and the street stalls had a variety of them. So I decided to buy whatever was easiest to carry.

I overthought things the last time the Man-God gave me advice. Just as an amateur cook adds too many ingredients to a dish, overthinking had landed me in a figurative shit pile. This time I was going to follow his advice exactly. I would brainlessly heed his instructions, buy the food he told me to, then just as brainlessly navigate my way through whatever event was going to happen in the back alley. This was roleplaying. Whatever occurred from here on would be completely unplanned. I wouldn't overthink anything; I would act as simple-mindedly as possible. That jerk liked entertainment. He was counting on me to overthink things again. As long as I didn't do that, he wouldn't be entertained.

Those thoughts preoccupied me as I wandered aimlessly for several minutes before suddenly realizing something. "Wait, this is exactly what he's expecting, isn't it?"

I'd been deceived! He led me on with his impressive smooth talk and now I was about to do exactly what he wanted me to do. When I realized that, it pissed me off. I was dancing right in the palm of his hand.

Remember his original intention, I told myself. *Remember how you felt the first time you met.* The Man-God wasn't someone I could trust.

All right then, this would be the last time I did as he told me. I would follow his advice and see how things turned out this time, but there was no way I would obey him next time. There was no way I was going to become his puppet and let him string me along! Period!

I marched down the alleyway. By myself, of course.

Why did I have to be alone, anyway? That was the key part of his advice this time. It must be something that Ruijerd and Eris wouldn't approve of. *No, don't overthink it*, I told myself. *If you want to think about something, then just think about how happy you'll be if it turns out to be something sexy.*

I had told Ruijerd and Eris that I would be off on my own for the day. It was dangerous to leave Eris to her own devices, so I entrusted Ruijerd with her protection. Maybe the two of them were off to see the beach right now.

"Wait...isn't that a date?" In my mind I saw the two of them together on the beach just before their silhouettes disappeared behind the shade of a large rock.

No, no, no! There's no freakin' way! J-just, just calm down, okay? This is Eris and Ruijerd we're talking about, right? This isn't some kind of sexual fantasy. It's nothing more than babysitting. Baby. Sitting!

Ah! But Ruijerd was really strong after all, and Eris seemed to respect him a lot! Lately she had been treating me like nothing more than a Kennel Master.

No, no, what the hell are you panicking over? I berated myself. *Deep breaths, everything is okay. Mister Ruijerd, you wouldn't steal her away from me, right? I have nothing to worry about, right? When I go back the two of you won't have mysteriously gotten closer to one another right? I-I trust you guys, okay?!*

In my head I simulated a fight between Ruijerd and myself. There was no way I could win in close-range combat. If I wanted to deal with him, I needed to start somewhere outside of his range of detection. Then I would have to use water to finish him off. He got in the way of our seaside fun, after all. I would attack him with water as retribution for that. If I produced a massive amount of water, I could sweep him all the way into the ocean. The end! He could drift at sea until he drowned. Mwahaha!

Wait, don't misunderstand me. I did trust Ruijerd. It was just that, well, you know that saying. Love is a battle-field, right?

It was quiet in the back alleys. Even the words "back alley" conjured the negative image of a bunch of un-scrupulous characters gathering in one place. In reality, tender and innocent boys like me were liable to get kidnapped for walking around a place like this. In this world, kidnapping was one of the most common forms of crime for earning money. Of course, if anyone was stupid enough to kidnap me, I would crush their arms and legs to torture their address out of them, then I would take everything of value in their homes before finally turning them in to the authorities.

"Heh heh heh. Little girl, if you come with me I'll give you enough food to fill you up."

As in on cue, a voice came filtering through one of the alleyways. I quickly peeked in its direction and spotted a shady-looking man pulling at the hand of a girl who was slumped against the side of a building.

It was easy to deduce what was going on. The one who moves first wins, however, so I readied my staff. Then I created a modified stone cannon with the speed and power of a boxer's jab and aimed it at the man's back. I had gotten good at limiting the power of my spells this past year.

"Yowch!!"

When he looked over his shoulder, I fired off another round. This time I strengthened it a bit.

"Gah!"

The spell rammed into his face with a violent thud, where it fragmented and crumbled to the ground. The man staggered and stumbled before collapsing. I was sure he wasn't dead. I had done a good job of restricting my power.

"Are you okay, young lady?" I tried to look as cool and collected as possible as I reached out to the girl who had almost been kidnapped.

"Y-yeah..." She was young and clad in a revealing black leather outfit: knee-high boots, hot pants, and a tube top. The pale skin of her clavicle, slender waist, belly button and thighs were all exposed. On top of all that, she had horns like a goat and voluminous, wavy purple hair.

With just one look I knew: She was a succubus. A young one at that. There was no question that she was younger than me. Perhaps this was the Man-God's way of rewarding me for my hard work. Maybe he had some sense in him after all.

No, wait, this wasn't a succubus. As far as I knew, there were no succubi among the demon races. If I remembered correctly, succubi inhabited the Begaritt Continent. Paul had had an unusually tense look on his face when he told me, "Our race has no chance against them." Even I would surely be powerless in the face of a succubus if I actually met one. Succubi were the natural enemy of the Greyrat family.

That aside, there were no monsters within the city. In other words, she was no succubus. She was just some demon kid in skimpy clothing.

"Y-you…you there, what have you…?" She was trembling like a fawn. "Th-this man is… He's…!" She had a look of utter disbelief on her face. A look of *oh gosh golly mister, what have you done?!*

"Ah, sorry. Did you know him?" I asked, tilting my head. The look on that middle-aged man's face didn't give me the impression that he was acquainted with this kid. If I were to describe it, it was more like the look of a man past his prime getting aroused by a little girl. Look at him, ruddy face contorted into a smile even though he was unconscious. I had no doubt he'd take her home and provide a lavish meal and put her in bed, but in return he'd expect a long, hot night.

"My belly aches from the hunger…and this man was going to provide me with a meal." A noisy, gurgling rumble punctuated her sentence, loud enough that it could have been the foreshadowing of an earthquake. When the noise stopped, the girl's knees gave out from beneath her and she crumpled.

"A-are you okay?" I knelt down and lifted her into my arms. She wasn't getting away. Don't get me wrong, though, the only reason I was there was to follow the Man-God's advice and save her. I wasn't of the same ilk as that pervert from a moment ago.

"Guh…urgh…it's been three hundred years since I

revived. Passing out in a place like this is inconceivable. Laplace can never know about this."

It felt like I'd stumbled onto the set of some mini-drama. Was this getup actually a cosplay or something?

"A-anyway, eat this and get some of your strength back." I crammed three of the fried skewers I'd bought into her mouth.

Munch, munch. The moment they entered her mouth, her eyes snapped open and stayed that way as she devoured the meat in seconds. Then she snatched the other skewers from me. I had a total of twelve, but in a snap of the fingers she had already eaten ten of them.

"Wh-whoa! Delicious! The first thing I've had in a year and it's so tasty!" The girl seemed to have recovered. She leaped into the air from her prone position, making a single rotation before landing on her feet. She was unexpectedly fit.

"A year? I don't know what your circumstances are, but that's a bit extreme." It wasn't as if she were a giant isopod that could live years without eating and not starve to death.

"Hm? Well, it's not like I counted the rise and fall of the sun, but with how empty my stomach was, it should be a close estimate."

Uh-huh. So she probably hadn't eaten in two days, then.

"Regardless, you saved me! You! I can surely last another year on this!" The young girl finally met my gaze. She had mismatched eyes, one purple and one green. This had to be another aspect of her cosplay. No, colored contacts didn't exist in this world, so maybe that was her natural eye color.

"Oh?" Her right eye spun around and turned blue. *G-gross!* "Whoa! Whoa! What's wrong with you, you're horrifically disgusting! What is this, what is it?! Ahahaha! I've never seen this before!" she shouted with far too much excitement as she looked at my face.

Uh yeah, needless to say that was a shock. It had been a long time since I last had someone look me in the face and call me disgusting. Then again, I'd just thought the same thing when I looked at her. So at least we were even.

"Could that be it? Were you a twin in the womb, but the other one died when you were born, is that it?"

...Huh? What the heck was she talking about? "No, I don't think anything like that happened."

"You're sure?"

"Yeah."

"But your mana pool... It's larger than Laplace's."

My what was bigger than who? I had no idea what she was talking about. From her weird way of speaking, to her freaky eyes, this kid was quite the disappointment.

"That aside, state your name!"

"Rudeus Greyrat."

"Very good! I am Kishirika Kishirisu! People call me the Great Emperor of the Demon World!" She proudly thrust her hips forward with her hands perched on her waist.

Her thighs appeared in front of me so suddenly that I stuck my tongue out without thinking.

"Aaaaah! What are you doing?! That's filthy!" She turned her toes inward and vigorously scrubbed her thighs together where I'd licked her, before glaring at me.

Still, now I understood. The Demon World's Great Emperor Kishirika Kishirisu was a name I'd heard before: the immortal Demon Emperor who led the demons in the Great Human-Demon War, only to meet a crushing defeat.

Was she the real thing? I had come here on the Man-God's advice, after all. There was a possibility that she really was who she claimed. Still, how could the real thing be here in a back alley of a city on the edge of the Demon Continent, on the brink of death from starvation? It just didn't seem likely, no matter how you spun it.

Ah, that's probably it, I realized. Children on this continent loved to pretend they were one of the great heroes of the past. The most popular of these figures was the Demon God Laplace. That was nauseating for me since

I knew the truth about him, but he was popular. Even though he lost the war, he successfully subjugated all the tribes on the continent and gave the people a fixed place to call home, thereby bringing them peace. He was regarded as one of the greatest demons in history. Children often played out his stories, particularly the episode where he fought with an immortal Demon King. That was the one I had seen numerous times on the way to Wind Port.

I supposed that the Great Emperor of the Demon World, Kishirika, was another one of the great people in history, but I'd never seen any children pretending to be her before. This girl had to be one passionate fan of the Great Emperor. And she had no friends to play with, which was why she was here by herself in a back alleyway like this. That was the most logical way to interpret the situation.

Hm. It was lonely, being all by yourself. I had no other choice, then. I had to play along. "A-ah, yes! How rude of me, Your Majesty!" I responded to her introduction with great exaggeration and took a knee as if I were one of her retainers.

"Oh? Ooh, yes! Very good, very good! This is the reaction I have been waiting for! Young people these days don't have any manners anymore, you see!" She nodded her head in satisfaction.

Yeah, knew it. She really wanted someone to play this out with.

"What a fool I was for not realizing you had revived. Please forgive me for my poor manners!"

"Very well. You saved my life. I will grant whatever wish you have, just one."

Her life? All I did was give her some food because she was hungry. "Um...how about an abundance of wealth!"

"Fool! You can see I'm penniless!"

But she said I could ask for anything! No, wait, maybe that was part of the act. Maybe there was some episode where someone asked the Great Emperor for money only for her to respond that she had none. "All right then, please give me half of the world."

"What?! Half of the world, you say?! That's enormous! Still, that's half-hearted. Why only half?"

"Oh, that's because I don't need the men." Oh crap, accidentally let my real feelings slip there. That wasn't something she was supposed to hear.

"I see, so that's it. You may be young, but you're a lecherous one. Still, my apologies. Even I haven't managed to take the world for myself."

True enough, Kishirika had lost every battle for the demons that she led. "All right, then I'm fine with your body. Please pay me with your body."

"Ohh? My body? For you to be that full of lust at your age gives me concern for your future."

"Ha ha, of course I'm just jok—"

As I tried to tell her that I was joking, she reached for her hot pants. "Oh well, I guess there's no help for it. This is my first time since I revived, so be gentle with me, all right?" Kishirika's cheeks burned bright as she slowly started to pull her pants down.

Huh? Seriously? I was just saying that as a joke. No, wait! Now it was too late to tell her that I'd only been joking. I would have to just observe as she revealed herself, and then afterward refuse by claiming that I was unworthy of Her Majesty.

"Ah, no, I mustn't do this." Before I could do that, Kishirika stopped herself. "I already have a fiancé. So sorry, but I can't do this." The skin she had exposed vanished as she pulled her pants up. It felt like she'd been toying with my poor, pure heart.

Anyway, so it was a no to money, no to the world, and no to her body.

"All right, then what *can* you do?" I asked.

"Fool! I am Kishirika, Great Emperor of the Demon World! It's obvious what I can bestow upon you! Demon eyes!"

So that was it. Well, I wasn't well-versed in the heroic

mythology of this world. Come to think of it though, didn't Ghislaine also have a demon eye?

"By 'demon eyes,' do you mean eyes that can see a person's lifeline? A line that, if cut, will kill the person with absolute certainty?"

"How horrific! What in the world is that power?! I don't have anything as terrifying as that!"

So that wasn't it. The only other sort of demon eye I knew of was the kind that turned the person you looked at to stone. I figured eyes which shot beams or lasers couldn't be considered demon eyes.

"For you to covet such a dangerous power... Tell me, do you hold that deep a grudge against someone?" she asked.

"No, not really."

"Nothing good comes of revenge. I've been killed twice, but I don't begrudge those who killed me now. A grudge is a chain that weighs you down. That's what started the Great Human-Demon War."

I was getting lectured by a little girl! Oh well, it's not like I had plans to target some vampire somewhere and slice them up. "To be honest, I don't really know much about demon eyes," I said. "What types are there?"

"Hm, as I've only recently revived myself, I don't possess any that significant, but there are Eyes of Magical Power, Eyes of Identification, Eyes of X-ray Vision, Eyes of

Distant Sight, Eyes of Foresight and Eyes of Absorption... Things like that."

Those were just names. "Can you explain to me what each of them do?"

"Hm? You mean you don't know? Honestly, young people these days don't spend enough time on their studies..." Despite these complaints, she proceeded to explain. "First, you have Eyes of Magical Power. With these you can see mana directly. These are the most common. One in ten thousand people possess one of these."

"Ah, the most popular then, huh."

"Eyes of Identification. You can use these to identify objects and their details. However, they can only give you information that I know. Anything I don't know will come up as unknown."

"I get it. Kind of like a dictionary, then."

She continued. "Eyes of X-ray Vision. These eyes can see straight through objects like walls. You can't see through living creatures or places with high mana concentration. But you could have your fill of seeing every girl naked. Perfect for a pervert like you, no?"

"As long as I'm not just seeing bones," I deadpanned.

"Eyes of Distant Sight. These can see things a great distance away. It's difficult to focus on things, though. While you can see things far away, you can't actually do anything to influence what's happening, so I wouldn't recommend these for you."

"No point in looking if you can't touch," I agreed.

"Eyes of Foresight. These can see things that will happen moments in advance. These are also difficult to focus, but these I would recommend."

"Businesses that like to stay one step ahead would love something like that."

"Eyes of Absorption. These eyes can consume mana. This includes mana that you use, so I don't really recommend them."

"Rinse and repeat, eh?"

Kishirika was very knowledgeable. She must have learned all of this somewhere. Perhaps her parents were well-educated. Or maybe there was a book about all the types of demon eyes out there.

"All right, then I'll take two so both my eyes can be demon eyes."

"You want two right from the start?" she asked. "You're greedier than you look."

"Come on, I'll give you another meat skewer."

I held out my last two skewers and she took them with a wide grin. "Yaay! Nom, nom…. You know, I don't mind giving you two demon eyes, but I don't recommend it."

"Why not?" I asked.

"You won't want to use them constantly. Most people generally cover their demon eye with an eyepatch. If you have two demon eyes, you won't be able to see at all."

"Ahh, now that you mention it, I know someone who uses an eyepatch." My sword master Ghislaine wore one. I later found out it wasn't because she had lost an eye, but because she had a demon eye.

"Also, a person who lives several hundred years might be able to control two demon eyes at once, but a child like you would lose your mind trying."

Lose my mind? So using them did have an impact on your brain. Scary. "All right, then let's not do two after all."

"That's for the best. Well, which will it be? I do recommend the foresight eye."

Demon eyes, huh? If I really were to obtain one, which would I rather have? I thought hard about each one of them, but they all had their uses. An eye for magical power seemed like a bit of a waste. It might come in handy, but then again, quite a few people seemed to have them. If I was going to get one, I wanted one that felt more unique.

I didn't really need an eye of identification. Not knowing what things are wasn't such a great inconvenience. Besides, anything the Great Demon Emperor didn't know would be listed as unknown, anyway. I could imagine it being useless just when I really needed it.

I didn't really need an Eye of X-ray Vision, either. It would take a while until I could properly control it, and I imagined having to see Ruijerd naked all that time.

The Eye of Distant Sight might be beneficial, but at the moment I had no desire for one. I could already guess what Ruijerd and Eris were up to without an Eye of Distant Sight, but if I had one I would probably see Eris threatening someone while Ruijerd tried to stop her.

As for the Eye of Foresight, I could certainly see why she recommended it. It was true that I couldn't beat Eris or Ruijerd in close combat right now. The creatures (and people) of this world were quick, after all. Being able to see into the future even for a few seconds would be a huge advantage to me.

The Eye of Absorption was completely out of the question. That would just kill the advantages I had as a magician. Still, it was good to know that such a demon eye existed. Otherwise I would have panicked if I came up against someone who could render my magic completely ineffective.

Oh well, it didn't matter which one I picked. We were just playing around, anyway. "All right, give me the one you recommended, the Eye of Foresight."

"Are you sure? Most people ignore my recommendations and choose something else for themselves, saying 'what's so great about being able to see a few moments into the future?'"

"If you can see even one second into the future, you can control the world." Even so, the swordsmen in this world were quick. I might not be able to beat them even with the power of foresight. There was the Longsword of Light, after all.

"Not the Eye of X-ray Vision, hm? No to seeing all the naked girls you want?"

This little girl sure didn't get it, did she? Sure, I could see the naked body of any beautiful girl or woman who walked by on the street and it would probably turn me on. But that was it. I would get fed up with that quickly. The process of imagining them undressing was what I enjoyed, anyway.

"I see, I see. All right, bring your face over here."

"All right."

"Here goes!" *Squelch*. She jammed her finger into my right eye.

A sharp jolt of pain shot through me. "Gyaaah!"

Instinctively I tried to retreat, but Kishirika caught hold of me. I couldn't move. She was stronger than I expected.

It hurts, it hurts, it hurts, my brain screamed. "Gaaaah! Wh-what the hell are you doing, you brat?!"

"Oh shut up. You're a man, aren't you? Bear with the pain a little!" She ground her fingers around in my eye socket as if she were tinkering with it, then pulled them out with a *pop*! I was left completely blind in that eye.

"The iris of the Eye of Foresight is a bit different than your normal color, but people won't be able to tell the difference from afar."

"You absolute moron! There's a difference between what is and what is *not* okay to do when you're playing around!"

"I'm the Demon World's Great Emperor. I wouldn't 'play around' about giving you a demon eye."

Dammit, my eye... My eye is... Aaaaaah—wait, what? I paused in confusion. I could see. Everything looked like it was doubled, though...? What the heck was going on? It was nauseating.

"Depending on how you supply mana to it, you should be able to make it as thin as possible. Well, do your best to learn how to use it."

"Huh? What? What are you talking about?"

"I'm saying it all depends on you." Kishirika seemed pleased with herself, no matter how confused her words left me. I saw an afterimage of her nodding, and within that afterimage was a thick shadow. What was it?

"Very good—so you can see it after all. Well then, I'll be on my way. I need to search out Badigadi. Much appreciation for the food."

Once she finished talking, she leaped through the air and landed on the roof above with a *thud*. "Fare thee well, Rudeus! Bwahahaha! Bwahahahah—gah!"

There was a doppler effect as she left, the sound of her high laughter gradually fading. I listened to it in blank amazement.

"Wait... She was the real thing?"

And that was how I obtained the Eye of Foresight.

CHAPTER 3

Missed Connections, the Sequel

A DEMON EYE. Most people would be shocked at receiving such a thing so suddenly. By chance, she happened to be in that alley, and by chance, she happened to give it to me. It was such a twist of fate, and my mind had not caught up with what was happening.

That aside, I had done just as the Man-God instructed me. So that meant things went exactly the way he wanted them to. The thought made me want to tear the eye out and crush it underfoot. I didn't, though, because that seemed too painful and scary.

At any rate, I started back to the inn and cursed my own naivety. The people walking around town were all doubled. Which was the future, and which was the past? Even if I could tell, people's movements were unpredictable. I kept misjudging them with my eyes and bumping into people.

"Tsk! Watch where you're walking!"

From the man's appearance, I guessed he was a small-time thug. He had a voluminous beard on his chin and a scar on his face. I didn't get the impression he was an adventurer, but rather one of the many pests that infested the city.

"Yes, I apologize. My eyes aren't very good."

"Your eyes aren't good, eh? Then walk on the side of the road! You know most of the folks around this area that can't see or hear well look apologetic when they're walking around!"

He was just trying to pick a fight. His threats were intimidating, but I could tell he wasn't that angry, just a bit irritated. "I'll be careful from now on," I said.

"That's right, watch it!"

I didn't want things to escalate further, so I just held my tongue and looked the other way.

The thug hocked and spat at the ground before walking off. Then he paused. "Tch...ah, that's right," he said. "I just have one question for you. You seen a drunk moron walking around here? He never came back yesterday."

I saw it just as he looked back at me: a flowerpot shattering right on top of his head. What happened next was instantaneous. I channeled mana with my right hand and released wind magic that blew him out of the way.

"Gah!" He somersaulted across the ground, then leaped to his feet in a defensive stance. He whipped out his sword and aimed its tip at me. "Bastard, what the hell are—"

That was when the flowerpot crashed against the ground, shattering. Both of us followed its trajectory upward. A middle-aged woman gazed down at us with a dumbfounded look upon her face. "I-I'm so sorry! Are you all right down there?"

"Ah, yes, we're fine!"

She ducked back into the house after I answered. The thug's gaze flitted between me, the spot where the pot had fallen, and his current position. He gulped.

"Umm...about that drunk guy, he's passed out in one of the alleyways. Probably had a fight with someone. Anyway, I'll be off." I spoke as quickly as possible before turning my back on the scene. I didn't want to be further involved with that thug.

This eye seemed to have its uses after all, though it would be a nuisance if it caused problems like this constantly. I decided to work on mastering it quickly.

I returned to the inn. When I told Eris and Ruijerd that I had met the Demon World's Great Emperor, they were both flabbergasted.

"The Demon World's Great Emperor? I didn't think she would revive." Ruijerd had a rare look of surprise on his face.

"And I never dreamed I would get something like a demon eye so suddenly."

"Bestowing demon eyes is a power only the Great Emperor possesses," he explained.

The Great Emperor of the Demon World, Kishirika Kishirisu, was also known as the Demon Emperor of Resurrection. Another name for her was the Demon Emperor of Demon Eyes. Apparently, she wasn't that skilled in combat, but with twelve demon eyes in her possession, there were many things she could see that most could not. Her most fearsome power was her ability to turn another person's eye into a demon eye. It was through that power that she bestowed demon eyes on all of her followers, giving her the power to rule over all of the demon tribes. There were even those who became her followers just so they could obtain more power.

"I wonder what she was doing in this city?" I said.

"Who knows? I have no idea what goes through the minds of Demon Kings or Demon Emperors," Ruijerd said with a shrug.

True, I thought. *You didn't even know the true intentions of the Demon God you served for so many years, after all.* Not that I would say as much to him, knowing it would only depress him.

Eris, on the other hand, was starry-eyed over the title "Demon World's Great Emperor." "That's incredible. I want to meet her, too!"

"You do?"

Eris and Kishirika. Just what kind of conversation would the two of them have if they were to meet? Even I was a little curious. As unlikely as it seemed, they might find common ground.

"I wonder if she's still in the city."

"I'm not sure," I said.

Who knows? Maybe if I went back through the alleys tomorrow, I'd find her passed out from hunger again. It felt like a highly plausible running gag, given her character. But still, quite unlikely. It seemed she was searching for someone, so she'd probably moved on already. It was as if she were a magical girl being led on by the Law of Cycles, or something. "I'm sure she's probably left the city by now."

"Really? That's too bad," Eris said. She would probably go check out the back alleys tomorrow anyway, despite what I said.

"Anyway, with that said, I'm going to hole up in the inn. You two are free to go off on your own."

They each gave a nod.

It took a week to learn how to use the demon eye. Put simply, it wasn't that difficult. You could control the eye through mana. It was very similar to the way I used magic without chanting, which I had done many times before. Through mana, you could control what you saw. I was confused until I realized there were two types of focus. Then things came together quickly.

One of the focus types controlled opacity, like changing the shade of dialogue windows in an erotic game. At first, it was turned to max, so everything appeared fully doubled. I made the opacity as low as possible. By channeling mana into the inner part of my eye, I could weaken my foresight ability enough to see the present. Glimpses of the future were beneficial, though, so I adjusted the opacity to the exact point where it wasn't distracting, but still visible. Then I tried to maintain it like that. If I lost focus for even a second, the opacity would change. It took three days before I could keep it consistent.

The next one was duration—or rather, the latency. I could change how far into the future I could see by channeling mana into the forefront of my eye. The furthest forward I could normally see was only one second, but with the use of mana I could see two or more seconds into the future. Things blurred into twos or threes, like the branch of a tree splitting off and representing different possibilities.

I could see up to three or four seconds with more mana, but if I tried to see up to five seconds in advance, the image split and blurred so much that it gave me a headache. That was representative of just how many ways the future could change. Also, the further you tried to see into the future, the more it taxed your brain, apparently. Kishirika even said that having two demon eyes would cripple you. Perhaps it was the influence of all her demon eyes that made her seem like such an airhead.

Regardless, I knew that I could safely see one second into the future. It took me three days to master this, then an extra day to learn how to control both factors at once. In total, it took seven days to learn the basics of using my Eye of Foresight.

While I was busy channeling mana into my eye and commanding it, *Do my bidding, Eye of Foresight!* Eris and Ruijerd went somewhere together every day. When they returned, Eris was always bathed in sweat while Ruijerd looked as composed as ever, only perspiring slightly more than usual. The two of them were doing something to work up that sweat. And every single day, at that!

"Just for the sake of reference, I'd like to ask. What are you two doing?"

Eris was wringing out a rag drenched in sweat when I asked. She answered, "Heh heh, that's a secret!" She looked to be truly enjoying herself.

So she was doing something in secret that she couldn't tell me? Oh, I get it. A little *afternoon delight*, eh? Guess my only hope for action was to drown myself in the scent of that sweat-soaked rag she was holding.

Don't get the wrong idea—I wasn't particularly worried about it. They were probably just going out and training. While her attitude might have suggested otherwise, Eris actually was the type to work hard in secret. Back when we were in the Fittoa Region, she did the same thing, frequently training with Ghislaine on her days off. Back then, whenever I asked her what she was doing, she would get that same overconfident smirk on her face and say, "It's a secret!" So I was sure it had to be training this time, too.

That night I had a dream about a thirty-four-year-old shut-in prodding me in the cheek as he whispered in my ear, "From now on your nickname will be 'pathetic loser.'" I figured it had to be the Man-God's handiwork. That bastard was really good for absolutely nothing.

A week later I informed Eris and Ruijerd about my ability to control the Eye of Foresight. When I did, Ruijerd suggested, "Then why don't you and Eris have a bout?" Was it to test how usable this thing was in battle? Or was it to show me the results of her special training? Accomplishing both at once would be a sweet deal, so I accepted.

We relocated to the beach. Ruijerd stood on the sidelines to observe while we took up positions opposite one another, swords in hand.

"Do you really think you can beat me now just because you got that demon eye?!" Eris was feeling particularly confident today. She must've learned some new technique or something this past week.

I wanted to keep that cheeky grin on her face. "Nope, it's fine if I lose. I just want to know how much I can see in the midst of battle with this eye, that's all." That was why I wasn't going to use magic today. I wanted to see the fruits of my own labor, as well. I adjusted my eye to be able to see one second into the future and the fight began.

"Hmph, that sounds just like something you would say, but..."

I could see what she was going to do even as she was still talking. *She's going to suddenly swing her left fist at me.* If I didn't have this eye, I wouldn't have been able to re-act in time. Eris was a natural when it came to launching preemptive strikes.

"Hah!"

"Oho!" I was able to dodge her attack. I countered by clapping the side of her face.

Then the next vision came. *Eris won't even flinch—she'll start an onslaught of attacks instead, with the sword in her right hand.* That was Eris' strong point. She could shrug off any number of attacks and launch right into an offensive. Her lower body was so strong that most attacks wouldn't send her reeling. In fact, the more damage she took, the more it charged her rage and the more aggressive her attacks became.

"Tah!"

"Okay!" I struck her forearm hard. Eris dropped the sword. Previously, I would have considered the battle over at that point. Dropping your sword meant you lost, or at least it did when I was training under Ghislaine. However, I could see with my eye that this wasn't over yet.

Eris is already falling back into her second line of attack.

In other words, this was just one of her feints. She dropped the sword to get me to lower my guard.

She'll punch me right in the chin with her left fist.

In other words, she purposefully dropped the sword to lure me into a false sense of security, so she could launch into her usual style of hand-to-hand combat: Eris' special Boreas Punch.

"Wha...!"

"Your legs are open." I hooked my foot around hers, knocking her off balance. Her fist swiped at empty air and she fell to the ground.

Still, it seemed the battle wasn't over.

She's going to catch herself with her hands, use the rebound and torque to turn, and latch onto my right leg.

"Uh-uh." I stepped back and at the same time brought my knees down, pinning her so she couldn't move.

Thanks to the way she'd contorted her body in a desperate attempt to bite me, Eris' body was all twisted. One arm was squashed beneath her, while one of her legs was bent toward her bottom. I wondered what she would do next, but all I could foresee was more struggling.

"That's enough," our referee called out.

Eris drooped as if the energy had been drained out of her.

Did I win? Did I actually win? This was the first time I had ever beaten Eris in close combat and without magic.

"I failed, huh..." Eris had a surprisingly tranquil look on her face when she gazed up at me.

I got off her. She stood up slowly and dusted the dirt off of her outfit.

She's going to punch me.

Eris' expression soured when I stopped her fist with my hand. "I'm going home!" she declared loudly. Her shoulders trembled as she left for the inn.

Did I really piss her off? I wondered. No, that wasn't it. I probably just made her lose some confidence. She'd always had an easy time beating me so far. Now I had suddenly gotten stronger. If I were in her place, I would have probably felt jealous, too.

"Eris is still a child," Ruijerd said as he watched her go.

"That's normal for her age," I responded before looking back at him.

He looked me in the eye and nodded. "Smooth work."

"Anyone who had a demon eye could do that."

I had gotten somewhat fitter, but there were dozens of other people in this world with similar physical ability.

Anyone who had a demon eye should be able to do the same.

"A demon eye isn't something a person can immediately master when they get it."

"Oh, really?"

"There was a Superd in my battle troupe who had a demon eye. He kept an eyepatch over it constantly and never managed to control it, not even till the day he died. You're an odd one for being able to control it after just one week."

Oh, okay. Okay, yeah. Yeah, I got what he meant.

Well, I did work really hard on controlling my mana flow, and I did master using it in just a week. So I was the only one able to control it this quickly, huh? I see, I see. Mwahaha! "Perhaps I could even beat you, Mister Ruijerd."

"If you use magic," he agreed.

"In close-combat?"

"Want to give it a try?"

I decided to take him up on that offer. To be frank, I was getting ahead of myself. "Yes, please."

Ruijerd put his lance aside and took a stance empty-handed. In other words, he didn't need his signature weapon against a runt like me. "You can use magic if you'd like," he said.

"No, if we're going to do this, we'll do it with our bare hands."

Before I had even finished, a vision appeared before me. *Ruijerd's palm is going to come straight at me.*

I could see it. I could see what he was going to do, and I could react to it.

"Oho!" I reached my hand out to stop him.

He's going to grab my hand.

The moment I saw the vision, I instinctively pulled my hand back. The next moment, the vision blurred.

He's going to catch me in the face with his fist.

Now there were two visions; in other words, two separate potential futures. One in which he grabbed my arm, and another in which he slammed his fist into my face. What was going on? Doubt stirred within me. My vision wasn't supposed to blur within a one-second window.

"Whoa!" I bent my body back, narrowly evading his attack.

Ruijerd's fist is going to come at my face.

I could see it. I could see it clearly. But my body was already contorted from dodging his last attack. Even if I could see what he would do next, I wasn't able to move in time to avoid it.

"Bwah!"

His fist caught me right in the middle of my face. My

head struck the sandy beach as I tumbled to the ground. I was left lying there facedown.

I reached a hand up to check for injuries. I was okay, right? I hoped he didn't completely mangle my beautiful face. I didn't have a pushed-in pug face now, did I?

"Yield?"

I could sense it was over the moment he asked that. "Yes, I admit defeat." I thought I could win when I saw the first vision, but it seemed things weren't quite so simple.

"But now you understand, right?"

I took the hand he held out to me and stood up. "No, I don't. The future I saw just blurred. How did you do that?"

"I have no idea what you saw, but I decided that if you tried to defend with your hand I would grab it, and if you didn't then I would punch. That was all that went through my head."

In other words, as long as he could guess what I was going to do next, he could react to it. There was such a gap in our skill levels that my ability to see one second into the future ultimately meant nothing. Similar to shogi, you could say. Even if a novice could see one move ahead, there was still no way they could beat a master.

The inhabitants of this world were, to an unusual degree, highly skilled. There were probably many others out there who could fight like Ruijerd.

"More importantly, I've fought someone with the same demon eye before. Ever since then, I've fought with the assumption that everyone has the same ability. You and I have different levels of experience."

"That's true."

So he used his experience to combat the Eye of Foresight. Perhaps the sword styles of this world also had ways to counter the power of a demon eye—for instance, the Sword God Style's Longsword of Light. I got the feeling that even if you could see it, you wouldn't be able to dodge it.

"It looks like I got a little ahead of myself."

It seemed the weaknesses of the demon eye were already long-established, such as finding a way to block the possessor's vision, using a shield, attacking from behind, or even fighting in the dark.

All that aside, this eye still had its appeal. I beat Eris, after all. Just thinking about the ways in which I could use it from now on made my heart pound. I had predicted everything Eris would do. A complete 180 from how things were before. In other words, with practice, I might even be able to predict Ruijerd's movements.

That was when the hermit appeared with a *poof* inside my head, with his bald head and sunglasses. "Now you don't have to get smacked around all the time to see how far you've come!" he said.

All right, then. Thank you, breast-loving hermit. Hmm. Thinking about all the ways I could use this eye really did make my heart soar!

When I returned to the inn, wearing a dreamy look on my face, I found Eris perched on the bed with her knees hugged to her chest. Oh, right, I had forgotten about her. She was depressed. Meanwhile, my inner hermit had hopped on his turtle and disappeared somewhere else.

"Um, Eris?"

"What do you want?"

After our battle, Ruijerd told me what the two of them had been doing this past week. Apparently it was special training, after all. Not the perverted kind, of course. To strengthen herself, Eris had dedicated every single day to sword practice. As a result, she had successfully managed to beat him one time.

She'd beaten Ruijerd once. That was extraordinary. I'd probably never manage that in my entire life. Apparently, Eris got pretty cocky because of it. That's why Ruijerd used me to deflate her ego.

Seriously, what the hell? It was his own mistake and yet that lolicon-loving wannabe warrior made me clean up his mess. Still, it was effective. Her ego had swelled so much after claiming victory against an opponent she'd never beaten before (Ruijerd), only to be punctured by losing to an opponent who had never defeated her before (me).

That said, I didn't think this was the right way of handling it. I knew what it was like to finally start thinking, *Hey, maybe I've got the hang of this?* only to be proven otherwise. It left you feeling completely miserable, as if everything you'd done up until now had been pointless.

Sure, perhaps it helped cool her head. Maybe she wouldn't make big mistakes now. But Eris was probably in a period of rapid growth. I didn't think checking her ego was the right answer. Instead, it was better to let her ride that high so she could develop even faster. Then you could point out her shortcomings and correct them afterward.

"You really have gotten very strong, Eris."

"It's fine, you don't need to comfort me. I knew I couldn't beat you, anyway." Still irritable, she stuck out her bottom lip in a pout.

Hmm, what could I say to her? I didn't have any good stock phrases for times like this.

Ruijerd hadn't come back to the room with me. It was his fault her ego got out of hand in the first place, so I wished he would do something about this, even though it was true that I was the one who had actually burst her bubble.

Then again, if I could comfort her properly, her affection meter would undoubtedly go up. She would fall head over heels for me, and the two of us would hold each other cheek-to-cheek in a love dance. Ruijerd must have assumed that was what would happen, and that's why he'd left us alone.

"Don't lose all of your confidence over this. I heard you managed to beat Ruijerd once. That's amazing, right?" I took a seat beside her as I spoke. When I did, Eris leaned her body against mine. The sweet scent of sweat filled my nostrils. It was a good smell, but I had to rein myself in. I needed to be a gentleman in this situation.

"It's cheating, Rudeus. You got a demon eye for yourself while I had to work my butt off..."

I froze. My head instantly went numb. My inner wolf receded with its tail tucked firmly between its legs. There was nothing I could say in response.

She was right. What was I getting so happy over? It *was* cheating. What I'd done was dishonest. The demon eye's power wasn't something I'd worked hard to obtain. It just fell into my lap. All I did was buy food from some stand and wander the back alleys. True, it had taken me a

week to master its powers. But that was it. I hadn't struggled at all. What the hell was I doing using that power and acting all happy that I'd beaten Eris when she spent an entire week working hard, drenched in sweat?

"I'm sorry."

"Don't apologize."

Eris went completely silent after that. She didn't move away from me, though. My heart would normally be pounding at her scent or the warmth of her body, but this time it didn't. Instead I just felt ashamed, as if her heat and the smell of her sweat were criticizing me. The air felt heavy.

Maybe it was better for me to not use the demon eye unless absolutely necessary. Its convenience might hamper my growth. I understood as much after fighting Ruijerd.

Right now, the most important thing wasn't thinking about how to utilize this demon eye. Instead, I needed to hone my combat ability. True, I was a better fighter when I used the eye. But my skills would eventually plateau if I relied on that. Relying on a crutch would only come back to haunt me later. It was dangerous. I almost let myself play right into the schemes of that treacherous devil, the Man-God.

I decided I would only use my demon eye as a final trump card.

That night I spent time thinking by myself.

Ultimately, we hadn't found a way to cross the ocean yet. Had I messed up somewhere? I followed the Man-God's advice well enough, but all I had gained was the demon eye.

Was this supposed to help somehow? Like with gambling? But pleasures like gambling didn't exist here on the Demon Continent. If they did, they were probably in the form of betting on brawls between two people. That wouldn't earn me much money. We could use Ruijerd as a gladiator and charge a participation fee of one crude iron with a prize pool of five green ore coins, but eventually he'd run out of opponents.

Hmm. No matter how much I thought about it, I couldn't come up with any solutions. We were still in the same situation as we were before I was given the Man-God's advice. In a way, we had wasted a week. Wasted an *entire* week.

"Okay…guess I should sell it." Saying the words out loud helped strengthen my resolve.

Fortunately Ruijerd wasn't around tonight, and Eris was already on the edge of her bed with her belly hanging out. It would be troublesome if she caught a cold, so I pulled a blanket over her.

There was no one to stop me. Surely the back alley pawnshop was still open, right? After all, shops that dealt with suspicious items were always open at night. With my staff in one hand, I left the inn.

I only made it three steps outside.

"Where are you going this late at night?"

Ruijerd was standing in my way. He hadn't been in the room, so I thought he was off somewhere else. Clearly, I was wrong. Dammit, what was he trying to do, peep on people? I had to fool him somehow.

"Um, I was just going to go have some sexy and danger-ous late-night fun at one of the brothels."

"And you need your staff to have sex with a woman?"

"Uh...it's a prop for sex play."

Silence. I knew that wasn't going to cut it.

"You intend to sell it?"

"...Yes." His aim was so precise I had to confess.

"I'm going to ask you again. Are you going to sell that staff?"

"Yes. This staff is made out of really good quality materials, so it should sell for quite a sum."

"I'm not talking about that. Isn't that staff important to you? Just like this pendant." He held up Roxy's pendant, hanging around his neck.

"Yes, it's just as important."

"If similar problems happened in the future, would you sell this pendant, too?"

I paused. "If it were necessary."

He took in a deep breath. I thought he was going to scream, even though he wasn't the type to raise his voice unless it had something to do with children. He didn't yell. Instead, he breathed out a sigh as he spoke. "I would never give up my spear, not even if I were driven against a wall."

"That's because it's a memento from your son, right?"

"No, because it's the embodiment of a warrior's spirit."

A warrior's spirit, huh? Those were elegant words, but they wouldn't get us across the ocean.

There was a sadness in Ruijerd's eyes. "You said we had three options before."

"I did," I agreed.

"I don't remember selling your staff being part of any of those options."

"It wasn't."

It seemed he was going to reproach me for lying to him. No, I never intended to lie. Selling my staff was a part of the frontal attack option.

"Have I still not earned your trust?"

"Trust? I trust you," I said.

"Then why won't you discuss it with me?"

I averted my eyes at the question. I knew he wouldn't approve of my plan. That's why I didn't talk to him about it. Perhaps you could say that was proof that I didn't really trust him after all.

"I believe I've come to understand the current state of the world in the past year. Even if we completed missions from the guild or went dungeon diving, we would never be able to save up two hundred iron ore coins. It's too much money."

Ruijerd was being unusually realistic in his speech tonight. Did he eat something weird?

"You knew that. That's why you came up with the option of using a smuggler. I wouldn't have thought of that. But that's the only way for me to get to the Millis Continent. You're correct about that. So why are you trying to sell your staff?"

The only thing I came up with was a better option, not the best option. The best option, the one where everything worked out perfectly, was too difficult and would likely end in failure. So I didn't know the correct solution, just as I hadn't any other time before. That was also why I wasn't convinced that using a smuggler really was the right option.

"Even if it is the right option, there's no point if it creates a rift within our party," I said.

"So you think that if we rely on a smuggler, it will create a rift?"

"Yes. Because according to your values, a smuggler is nothing more than a criminal."

Smuggling... Slaves were included in the list of goods they carried. Plus, one of the more popular crimes in this world was kidnapping. Children were easy to kidnap. Put simply, smugglers were accomplices to kidnapping and selling children.

"Rudeus."

"Yes?"

"It's my fault that things have come to this. If it were just the two of you, you wouldn't have to worry about getting two hundred green ore coins."

On the other hand, if he hadn't been with us, we might have met with disaster on the way here. Ruijerd had helped us a countless number of times.

"Even if you solve the problem by selling your staff, my pride can't accept that."

His pride didn't change what needed to be done.

"If I sell the staff, I'll get the money. Then we can play by the rules, pay, and cross the sea. No one has to have any regrets. No one has to compromise anything. That's the smartest way to go about this, right?"

"But the shame I will feel because you sold it will still remain. Eris will be bothered by it, too. Isn't that the rift that you were talking about avoiding?"

I went silent as Ruijerd looked straight at me.

"Look for a smuggler. I'll turn a blind eye to their crimes." He had a serious look on his face. He'd probably resolved not to interfere even if he encountered an abducted child, just so I wouldn't have to sell my staff. It was all for my sake. He was bending his own principles and beliefs for my sake. If his resolve was that strong, I couldn't argue the point with him.

"If, during the trip, you see a real sleazebag and you can't hold back, please tell me. We should at least be able to help a child."

If Ruijerd was that serious about it, then I would drop this plan, however smart I thought it was. We would rely on a smuggler to cross the sea. But this time I wasn't going to cater to other people. If Ruijerd couldn't hold himself back, we would betray them without hesitation and help whoever needed it. We would use the criminals as needed and then toss them aside.

"All right, then let's start looking for a smuggler," I said.

"Yeah. Let's do that."

"I'm afraid you'll see a lot of unpleasant things along the way, but let's get through it together."

"Same to you."

The two of us exchanged a firm handshake.

We released our hands and were about to head back in to sleep when Ruijerd's face went rigid. He suddenly readied the spear in his hands. "Who is it?! What business do you have here!"

I trembled with surprise at how sudden and intimidating his actions were, then followed his gaze. There, in the darkness of an alleyway, was the figure of a lone man with a half-smile on his bearded face. He had his arms raised as if to demonstrate that he had no ill intent. A sword hung at his side. He looked like he'd walked right out of a combat scene in a movie.

"Ooh, scary. Here I thought everything I'd heard about the Superd race was a load of crap, but here you are, the real thing." He wore a faint smile as he approached. I had seen this guy somewhere before. "First off, could you put away that dangerous-looking weapon? Not like I came here looking for a fight. I was searching for you so I could give you my thanks."

"This late at night?"

"Little early for you to be off in dreamland, no?"

Ah, I remembered now. This was the man I tangled with previously, the guy whose shoulder I bumped into after receiving my Eye of Foresight. I never dreamed he would come to thank me in the middle of the night. He really was a thug.

"Took me a little while to find you. No one knew about any magicians with bad eyesight. But when I heard the rumors about Dead End, I knew it was you. Your gray robe and ability to cast spells without chanting anything, as well as your height—short as a hobbit—and that condescendingly polite way of talking."

I wasn't actually a hobbit, though.

"Kennel Master Ruijerd. You helped me seven days ago. And thanks to you I also found that moron, as well. When I found him, he had his chin smashed in and was collapsed in an alleyway. Poor fool. In the state he's in, he won't be able to drink anything but alcohol for a while. Not that he ever drank anything else, anyway."

Seriously?

"Nah, I was just joking. I do at least have one healing magician among my friends."

Good. The man I bumped into might have been a pervy old lolicon, but at least he didn't have his jaw split open too.

"So is that what you came here to thank me for?"

"That, and for using your magic to push me out of the way. You saved my noggin from getting busted."

"So that's all. Well, glad to hear it."

The man spoke with extreme gravity. "In my line of work, there's nothing worse than a debt of gratitude. No matter how small it is, if you don't pay it back it'll eventually catch up with you, and you may get stuck in a situation where you have to betray your comrades. That's why it's best to pay it back and pay it back quickly." He shook his head dramatically and pointed at me. "I was listening in, Kennel Master, and you're in luck. It just so happens you bumped into someone who's a member of a smuggling organization."

Ruijerd and I turned to look at one another. This guy was a member of a smuggling organization? What a convenient development. I would've suspected him of lying, but there was also the Man-God's advice. Perhaps the whole point was so I would meet this man.

As I struggled to make a decision, the man seemed to misinterpret our silence and extended his palm toward us. "That said, don't get the wrong idea. I'm returning a favor, but smuggling a Superd is on a completely different level. I don't think my life is worth two hundred green ore."

Unsure of what he meant, I turned my eyes to him and encouraged him to continue.

The man just grinned. "I expect Dead End to be pretty strong, so I got a favor. Feel like listening?"

He was going to return a favor, but also wanted one of his own? That seemed a bit off. Then again, he did see me using magic without chanting. His talk of repaying a debt was probably just a cover; he was actually looking for someone competent to do a job for him. That was why he made his appearance when he heard our conversation.

Ruijerd cast a glance at me. Negotiating was my job, after all.

"It depends on the details of your request."

"Nothing too difficult." Yet the conditions he listed were a bit unexpected. "You see, we have to store smuggled goods before we deliver them, and then we have to keep them safe until the claimant comes to retrieve them. In a month from now, we're going to store some, ahem, *goods* before shipping them. I want you to release those people. If possible, I'd like you to make arrangements so they get back to their homes."

"Isn't that the exact definition of betraying your friends?"

"Nah, it's for their own good. There's one mixed among those goods...well, slaves, as you'd call them...who will cause trouble for us in the future. Selling them would net us a huge fortune, but it would also come back to haunt us a year from now." He shrugged and continued. "I tried to tell them no, but it's not like we're a single, organized group. I was looking for someone both capable and tight-lipped who could squash their plans. So how about it?"

Once again Ruijerd and I traded glances. We weren't kidnapping, but rather saving people. If that were the case, I didn't see the problem with it, but...

"Why can't you do it? With your sword and your abilities, you should be able to, right?"

"That's right. I may not look it, but I'm the strongest among my buddies. Still, Mister Superd, it's not like I wanna betray my comrades. I have to consider what would happen afterward, you understand. Even if I saved them, I'd have nowhere to go anymore, so there'd be no point. Just because you're the strongest doesn't mean you get to be on top."

"..."

From the look on Ruijerd's face, it was difficult to tell whether or not he understood where the man was coming from. He looked like he understood it on a logical level, but not an emotional one.

"Rudeus, I don't mind. You decide."

Ruijerd had just said he would close one eye to any wrongdoing. No matter how seedy the man in front of us was, he would obey if I decided to do it.

I considered it. A lot of this was suspicious. Still, this was something that transpired as a result of the Man-God's advice. While it was true that I couldn't trust the god himself, I was probably best off not overthinking things and going with the flow, just like I did last time.

Based on what we'd heard, we wouldn't be committing any crimes. There was a good chance the person we were helping was a horrible monster, but saving someone was still saving someone, regardless of their character.

Besides, we could really use a smuggler to lead us across the ocean. This wasn't a bad deal if we could cross without any charges or fees in return. With all that, it was easy to come to a decision.

"All right, we'll do it."

Ruijerd nodded and the man laughed. "All right then, I'll trust you to do a good job. Name's Gallus Cleaner."

"Rudeus Greyrat."

And so it came to pass that we exchanged names and decided to take on a mission from a smuggling organization.

Missed Connections, Extra Story

ROXY MIGURDIA, the woman who was Rudeus' master, ended her sea voyage in the city of Wind Port on the Demon Continent.

She stopped short as soon as she disembarked. Wind Port's townscape was much like that of Millis' northern city, Zant Port. Even those laying their eyes on it for the first time would be beset with a sense of déjà vu.

However, déjà vu wasn't the reason why Roxy paused. It was because there was a clear difference in the air here compared to Millis Continent.

It's been so long, she thought. Nostalgia rose from the depths of her chest. When was the last time she was here? It must have been about fifteen years ago. Now that she thought about it, she realized how much time had passed since she started envying the humans and fled from her village.

When she landed in Millis Continent's Millishion back then, and ate the sweets made by humans, she was shocked at how such delicious food could exist in the world. She decided then that she would never eat food from the Demon Continent again, and that she would never return, either.

A bit simple-minded, if I do say so myself, she thought.

In truth, she hadn't returned since she left Millis Continent for the Central Continent, and she'd never even considered going back. There was so much on the Central Continent. Everything she saw there was fresh and exciting, and before she knew it she'd already lived on the Central Continent for as long as she'd lived on the Demon Continent.

In all that time, the Demon Continent never crossed her mind. Not even when she went burrowing into labyrinths and faced death did she stop to think of the parents she'd left behind on the Demon Continent.

Despite that, now she had returned.

You never know where life will take you, she thought.

"Roxy! We're going!"

As she stood there, a woman called out to her. The woman's ears peeked out from a mane of luxurious golden hair the color of freshly baked bread. She was an elf, tall and slender with a small waist and a nice, round behind. Roxy's heart filled with envy every time she saw the woman from a distance. There was nothing she could do about it; it was how the elves were, but she still wished she could have a body like that. And while their busts were similar, the elf woman was well-balanced and beautiful, whereas Roxy looked plain and childlike.

"Yeah, I'm coming." A sigh escaped her lips.

The name of that magnificent woman was Elinalise Dragonroad. She was an elf warrior, a vanguard on the front line. She was equipped with a shield and an estoc, which she used primarily for thrust attacks. Her skills were just as magnificent as her appearance.

An estoc wasn't a common weapon amongst adventurers. In the Asura Kingdom, it was used by the nobles during duels, and in the northern region it was used by warriors when they were fully decked out in armor. The one in Elinalise's possession was a magic item found in the depths of a labyrinth. It was sturdier than most swords and a single wave could create a wind vacuum that could cut down trees meters away. The buckler was also a magic item with the ability to mitigate any attack it received.

"O-ooh...solid land, it's solid land..." An elderly dwarf came tottering out of the ship from behind Roxy. His heavy armor clanked and his grim beard swayed as he clung to his cane, his face ghostly pale.

His name was Talhand. Formally, he was known as Talhand of the Harsh, Large Mountain Summit. He was about Roxy's height, with more than twice the girth. This man, with his grim beard and heavy armor wrapped around his entire body, was a magician.

Why was a magician wearing so much armor? Even Roxy questioned it at first. But Talhand's feet were slow, and his agility nonexistent. If a beast attacked him, he had no way of evading it. However, with such bulky armor protecting him, he could use magic right on the front lines.

"Are you all right, Mister Talhand? Should I cast healing on you?"

"No, it's not necessary." He rocked his head back and forth and scooted his sluggish body forward. He was normally a bit more nimble than this, but he'd gotten seasick and it had weakened him.

Elinalise put her hand on her hip and harrumphed. "Seriously? How pathetic. It's *just* a boat."

Talhand's face went red with anger. "You... what did you just say...?!"

These two were quick to start fights with one another, so it fell to Roxy to intervene. "Let's fight about this later, please. Miss Elinalise, you don't have to comment on everything. Some people are predisposed to getting seasick."

Roxy had met them at the city of East Port in Dragon King's Realm. The two of them were fighting in the Adventurers' Guild, and at first, Roxy ignored them. However, she intervened when she heard amidst their bickering that they were searching for people who had gone missing from the Fittoa Region, and they planned to travel to the Demon Continent. Neither one of them was good with the geography of the Demon Continent, and had conflicting opinions as a result. Talhand argued that they should go to Begaritt Continent since they knew the lay of the land, or the northern part of the Central Continent. Elinalise, on the other hand, said they could still search for people even if they didn't know the way, and they could always hire someone once they arrived. And there was Roxy, dealing with her anxiety alone, a native of the Demon Continent. It was almost as if she were fated to meet them.

As their conversation continued, she found out they were former members of Paul and Zenith's party. Black Wolf Fangs, they were called. Roxy had heard of them. They were one of the most famous parties in all of the Central Continent: a mismatched party full of members with one or two odd quirks which was once talk of the town. They rose to S-rank in a few short years and disbanded shortly after, but Roxy remembered them well.

Still, she'd never realized that Paul and Zenith were members of the Black Wolf Fangs. She couldn't hide her surprise. And the two of them were just as surprised by her. After all, she was Roxy Migurdia, well-known by the people as a Water King-tier magician, a young blue-haired girl who hailed from the Demon Continent. She'd entered the University of Magic and within a few years obtained the title of Water Saint-tier Magician, then traversed a maze on Shirone Kingdom's outskirts that was twenty-five levels deep. After that, she took her seat as one of the Shirone Kingdom's court magicians.

A troubadour sang stories of her early adventures, turning them to verse that spread her name further. It was a story about how a young female magician left her hometown, encountered three novice adventurers, and traveled around the Demon Continent before setting off for the Millis Continent. Her name didn't appear in the rhyme. However, adventurers who knew the song recognized that it was Roxy from her description.

Calling the three of them (Roxy, Elinalise and Talhand) a group of kindred spirits would have been an overstatement, but it was true that their objectives coincided. Roxy was headed to the Demon Continent to search for Rudeus, while the other two were honoring Paul's request to search for his family members. And so they formed a party together and headed off to the Demon Continent.

The boarded a ship with Millis Continent as their first destination. There, in the city of West Port, they used an enormous amount of money to purchase Sleipnir horses and a carriage. A big expense, but little problem given the size of their purses.

They avoided the holy capital of Millishion, since the other two didn't get along with Paul terribly well. Both also had a bad reputation among their respective kin, so they kept away from the Blue Wyrm Mountain settlement where the dwarves resided, as well as the elf settlement in the Great Forest. Instead, they headed straight for Zant Port.

According to the pair, the rainy season would soon be upon the Great Forest, so they should move fast while they could. But with the way they forced the horses to move constantly, even at night, it seemed like they just didn't want to be on the Millis Continent for a second longer than was necessary. Roxy assumed the real reason was that they simply didn't want to go back home.

Whatever their reasons, they arrived on the Demon Continent in record time, so Roxy had no complaints.

"Let's head to the Adventurers' Guild first," Roxy proposed, and the three of them started in that direction. The guild was always a first stop for adventurers.

"I hope it's a nice place!"

Roxy pulled a face at Elinalise's words. The elf may have appeared chaste, but she *loved* men. It was hard to imagine with that figure, but she'd probably had numerous children. According to her, this was all a part of the curse that had been set upon her, but she didn't act the least bit aggrieved about it. In fact, she rather seemed to enjoy it. Roxy couldn't believe it.

"Miss Elinalise, we're not searching for men."

"I know that."

No, you don't, Roxy scowled. Elinalise might not have had any problem with her so-called curse, but Roxy wished she would think of the party she was traveling with. It was fine for Elinalise to do whatever she liked in her own time, but this was an emergency. Besides, if she got pregnant, it would only delay their trip even further.

I wish you'd take it easy a little, Roxy thought.

"Maybe you should get a man or two yourself and—"

"I can't do that."

Maybe if I looked as gorgeous as you, Roxy thought bitterly. Unfortunately, none of the men that Roxy had ever taken an interest in saw her as a woman. She was popular with children, but she had no luck when it came to men.

The Demon Continent's Adventurers' Guild had a unique feel to it compared to its counterpart on the Central Continent. Many different races were paired together in parties.

When Roxy entered, she chanced upon a group who were very clearly newbies. Three young boys, all dressed in warriors' gear. They approached her timidly.

"U-um, would you maybe...form a party with us?!"

Roxy smiled wryly in the face of their plea. "No, as you can see, I'm already in a party."

The three of them smiled bitterly at her refusal before making their retreat. It wasn't the first time she'd been invited to a party like this; she'd been asked numerous times by groups of three young boys. The troubadour had told her he would write songs of her, but she never expected to become this famous.

"Will you look at that, Roxy? You're getting invited by some fine boys after all!" Elinalise patted her on the head.

This happened often. Roxy wasn't going to bother responding to it. She wasn't a child. "Our ranks are too far apart. We couldn't form a party, anyway." Roxy was currently A-ranked. Boys beguiled by the troubadour's song were, on average, only D-ranked. She'd never been approached by any who were above Rank B.

The first time she got one of those party invitations, she bragged about how she was the main character in those songs, only to discover she wasn't actually named in them, thus embarrassing herself. It was a memory she'd prefer to forget.

She never imagined the troubadour would fail to recognize her race. Instead he wrongly assumed that she was only twelve and had become A-ranked in a mere two years. Not only that, but the current version of the song was so overdramatized that it said she traveled the Demon Continent and became A-ranked in only a year.

Don't kid yourself, Roxy thought. In reality, it took her about five years to rise to Rank A. With the Demon Continent as her base of operations, she rose to Rank B in three years. From there, she spent two years hopping from party to party. That was still a quick rise, though. If she were to start over from Rank F, she might be able to obtain an A-ranking in just a year, but a party of kids with no experience could never swing that.

"You could have shaped them into men who would suit my tastes. What a shame."

Elinalise's words triggered a flashback to the three novice adventurers who had first approached her back then. They called themselves the Rikarisu Gang, three young boys who helped her out after she left the Migurd village, when she was nothing more than a countryside bumpkin who couldn't tell left from right.

One of them was very sarcastic, always making up lies on the spot, but really good at looking out for people. Another loved to curse people out and had a foul mouth, but was also very determined. The third was incredibly clever, and the one who held the group together. He died during their journey.

Their party had disbanded when they reached Wind Port, but she wondered. Were the other two still alive and well? After adventuring on the Central Continent, she understood just how severe the conditions were here on the Demon Continent. There was a high chance they were already dead.

Nokopara and Blaze... I hope they're still doing well. She found herself laughing when she thought that. It had been twenty years. The two of them didn't have particularly long life spans, so they might have retired from adventuring long ago. The only one who'd stayed the same was her.

Let's leave the nostalgia for some other time, she decided, cutting her reminiscing short. She was here to find Rudeus or his family.

"All right, let's start gathering information," she proposed to the other two, and started scanning the inside of the guild.

From the information they gathered, they found out that Dead End was in this town—part of a new, up-and-coming group of adventurers who had quickly made a name for themselves.

Dead End. There was no person on the Demon Continent who didn't know that name. Even among the Superd, they were considered particularly dangerous, beasts that targeted mainly children. When Roxy was just a child, her mother often threatened her with that name. "If you don't behave, Dead End will come and steal you away," she would always say.

They returned to the inn. Roxy's face soured once they pooled all the information they had about this "Dead End".

"It's a bit difficult to believe."

"What part?"

"Hard to believe anyone in their right mind would pretend to be Dead End."

What was it about Dead End that was so terrifying? The fact that the actual group existed. Those on the Central Continent didn't know of it, but the name definitely referred to *someone* out there. Of course, Roxy had never seen them herself, but all the rumors she heard were terrifying. They were the most terrifying creatures on the Demon Continent.

The Adventurers' Guild had never listed their name exactly, out of fear of retaliation, but if there was an extermination request for those demons, it would most definitely be S-ranked. It was the type of job that would net an adventurer an instant S-ranking if they completed it.

"I haven't a clue, either," Elinalise said.

According to the information she'd gathered, the man claiming to be with Dead End was fair-skinned, bald, and carried a spear with him. He was also said to be very handsome.

"Since they said he's a good-looking guy, why don't I invite him to my bed to get some more answers?"

Talhand hocked and spat in disdain. "That info's useless."

According to what Talhand had gathered, Dead End was a group of three people. They referred to themselves respectively as Mad Dog Eris, Guard Dog Ruijerd, and Kennel Master Ruijerd. The latter two were brothers. The Mad Dog had red hair, the Guard Dog was a beanpole, and the Kennel Master was a midget. The Mad Dog used a sword, the Guard Dog used a spear, and the Kennel Master used a staff that was apparently a magic item. They didn't have a particularly good reputation.

"The Mad Dog is quick to lose her temper, and the Kennel Master's done nothing but awful things. Apparently, the Guard Dog isn't a bad guy, though. Loves kids, has a strong sense of justice and refuses to turn a blind eye to evil."

That's a very strange assessment for people to make, Roxy thought. Perhaps the group had started those rumors themselves. If a party of miscreants did something good, it would spread like wildfire. Apparently, they weren't just violent, but canny about it as well.

"A dangerous bunch. Let's be sure to avoid them."

"Aye," the dwarf agreed. "We don't need to be drawing the attention of the wrong sort when we're supposed to be looking for people."

"All right, then let's move on to the main agenda," Roxy said, redirecting the conversation. Their purpose in heading to the Adventurers' Guild hadn't been to glean information about Dead End. "Were there any rumors about people from the Fittoa Region?"

"Not one," said Talhand.

"No, I didn't hear anything," said Elinalise.

We must be too late, Roxy thought.

The Demon Continent was not the kind of soft place that one could survive being teleported to without the proper equipment. It was a land where simply surviving a year could prove difficult for locals. Also, it had already been a year since the Fittoa Region displacement. Those who were teleported might have all perished already.

"The ones we're really searching for are Paul's family."

"So Zenith, Lilia, Aisha, and Rudeus."

Roxy had taught Talhand and Elinalise how they might identify each one of them. Aisha was the only one she was vague about, because she only knew about her through Rudeus' letters.

"Well, Zenith should be just fine," Elinalise said.

"No doubt about that."

The two of them knew Zenith, so they expressed no concern. Roxy, on the other hand, didn't know how capable Zenith was, but she trusted in these former members of the Black Wolf Fangs who vouched for her. If Elinalise and Talhand thought Zenith would be fine, then she would be fine.

"Rudeus also stands out, so we should be able to find him immediately." Roxy remembered the overwhelming talent that her five-year-old pupil had demonstrated. He would surely be the talk of the town no matter where he went.

Zenith and Rudeus would be the easiest to find if they dug for information. They also had the strength to survive on the Demon Continent as long as they landed somewhere close to civilization. That was why they prioritized finding information on Lilia and Aisha from the start.

"Let's set a deadline. Two days to gather as much information on Lilia and Aisha as we can, then on the third day we make preparations to hit up other settlements in the area. Does that sound like a plan?"

"Isn't that a bit too soon?"

Roxy shook her head at Elinalise's words. "There's a high likelihood they're already dead, and the Demon Continent is big. We'll make a single pass through the major cities and submit missing persons requests at each guild along the way."

The Asura Kingdom would cover costs incurred while searching for residents of the Fittoa Region. As long as their group submitted requests at each guild, the reward for successful completion would be provided by the Asura Kingdom, so they could leave that for adventurers to pursue. It wasn't an automated process, because the guild required someone to sign a request form before they could post it. On the other hand, if the guild didn't post those requests, then Asura Kingdom had no reason to pay the guild.

Roxy felt genuinely irritated by how atrociously the Asura Kingdom was handling such a widespread disaster.

It was a major power, so she thought they should be taking more proactive actions. In truth, the only people actually participating in the search endeavors were Paul and those connected to him. In other words, only those affected by the disaster.

Looks like all that talk about the Asura Kingdom's inner circle being corrupt was more than rumor, she thought. It was the country with the longest history in the world, so it was still hanging on even as its traditions and power deteriorated.

"All right, tomorrow let's busy ourselves with gathering information."

"Okay, will do!"

"Roger."

Roxy wasn't the type to linger over things. No matter where she stayed, she never wasted any time. She always finished things quickly and then set off. That part of her personality showed up when she initiated Rudeus, teaching him her special technique and then immediately setting off again. Making swift decisions was her forte, but also part of why Rudeus saw her as an airhead. Others had pointed it out to her, but Roxy still considered it a strength.

That was why she settled on a schedule of submitting a request to the guild on the first day, searching around on the second, and setting off by the third. A prompt, concise schedule to be sure. If they had stayed for a week, the results may have been a little different.

On the second, Roxy's curiosity got the best of her and she went to go see what Dead End was up to. Their group stood out, so it was easy to find them.

A pair were training diligently on the beach. Just as her information said, one was a bald beanpole while the other was a young red-headed girl. She wielded her sword in both hands with such purpose, swinging it at a frightening speed while the bald man parried the attacks easily.

Her information said Dead End was a three-person group with one tall person and two small people. *Looks like the tiny Kennel Master isn't with them*, she thought.

The Guard Dog and Mad Dog continued their high-speed clash of offense versus defense. Perhaps *clash* wasn't the right word, given that the Guard Dog simply deflected the Mad Dog's attacks, but the techniques he used were beyond Roxy's level.

Roxy watched them from afar, peeking from behind the shadow of a boulder. It was almost as if this were pro baseball and she was the older sister of a pitcher who used balls of magic as their weapon in battle.

The two of them were strong, even to Roxy, who had traveled across the world as an adventurer. That wasn't strength which could be achieved through technique alone.

It might be good to make contact with them after all.

As soon as she thought that, the Guard Dog looked over his shoulder.

Ah...!

It felt like their eyes met. His gaze was so intense that it gave Roxy an unspeakable sense of terror. Enough to give her the illusion that she was prey being hunted.

She slipped away hastily.

Ruijerd sensed her from the very beginning. He wasn't sure what she wanted, or if she was just watching. When he casually looked in her direction, he saw a girl's face peeking out from behind a rock.

No, not a young girl, he realized. An adult Migurd female. He couldn't tell from a glance, but there was no fooling Ruijerd's third eye. He didn't recognize her presence, and there was also more than one Migurd settlement.

He figured she was probably just watching out of curiosity, but when he looked back, she turned away and ran off somewhere. *Hm. Did I scare her away?* he wondered.

He'd let his guard down momentarily, and Eris dove in. It was an attack with power behind it.

"Guh!"

After exchanging three blows, Eris struck Ruijerd on the back of his hand and made him drop his sword.

"Yay! Did I do it?! I did it, right?! Yeaaah!" Eris pumped both hands in joy.

Lately, her skills were beginning to take shape. In the future she would surely be a fine swordswoman, but right now she was still young. If she thought too much of herself now, it might spell disaster in her future. He hadn't planned to let her win a fight for a while, but that Migurd girl had caught his attention and he let his guard down for a moment.

Ruijerd let out a sigh, quietly enough so that Eris wouldn't hear it.

Roxy looked over her shoulder countless times as she hurried back toward the inn. The whole time, she worried that she was being followed and that an attack might be coming. If she was going to fight someone of that caliber, she needed to prepare a magic crystal. She might even need a magic circle drawn in a scroll.

It didn't seem like they would attack just because she'd been watching them, but if they were crazy enough to call themselves Dead End, Roxy wanted to be prepared.

"Aah! Yes! Right there! Harder, harder!"

Roxy felt exasperated when she heard the moans from behind Elinalise's door. The elf hadn't even bothered with gathering information; she simply found a man to bring to the inn so she could enjoy herself.

"Seriously...?"

Roxy had heard about Elinalise's habit of bringing men to her room from Talhand. No matter their circumstances, Elinalise would always fall for some man she met and spend the night with him. That included their time in Zant Port. According to Talhand, she even did this when they were in the depths of a labyrinth. The woman had no principles.

At the same time, Roxy felt somewhat relieved. She would have felt helpless if she'd been left alone. As long as Elinalise was in the neighboring room, she could prepare herself for battle and wait for her. Once the elf was done, Roxy would seize her by the ear and head out to resume gathering information together. That way she could also keep her eye on the elf, effectively killing two birds with one stone.

Although I doubt they would come all the way to the inn,

Roxy thought, as she entered her room to conduct battle preparations.

The walls weren't particularly thin, yet she could still hear Elinalise's moans filtering through. Listening to them put Roxy in a weird mood herself.

No you don't, she thought, and grabbed her right hand with her left just as it was reflexively reaching south. She didn't have the luxury of time for that right now.

They've been at it for a long time, she thought when three hours had passed. Roxy had continued to wait quietly. There seemed to be no end in sight for Elinalise's tryst. Granted, there was also no indication that Dead End was going to launch any attacks on them, either.

Roxy felt like an idiot. Not only could she not do what she needed, but she also couldn't express her frustration at Elinalise for being so selfish. It was especially infuriating since, unlike the elf, Roxy was showing self-restraint and telling herself that now wasn't the time to get busy.

When her anger hit its peak, Roxy finally busted down Elinalise's door. "Just how long are you going to keep this up! We're supposed to be gathering—"

"Oh, my! Roxy? When did you get back?"

"Ah...oh?"

There were five men in the middle of the room.

"Would you like to join in?"

There was a strong male odor. The men all had vulgar smiles, and Elinalise was mounted atop one of them, looking as if she were in the throes of ecstasy. The fact that there were multiple people, and that they were all consenting to this, was beyond Roxy's comprehension.

"Uh, wha..."

The scene before her was so reprehensible that Roxy couldn't process it.

"Aaaaaaaaaaaaaah!"

Roxy let out a futile scream as she scuttled out of the room. She flew into the adjacent one, completely out of breath and took hold of her staff.

"O spirits of the magnificent waters, I beseech the Prince of Thunder! With your majestic blade of ice, slay my enemy! Icicle Blast!"

The inn was left partially destroyed.

They set out from the town on the third day. They'd barely managed to gather any information after everything that happened, and they forgot to submit a request to the guild. They also destroyed an inn, which cost them a considerable amount.

"This is all Miss Elinalise's fault."

"You can't blame me. I was in a back alley gathering information when they came to me with their passionate appeal."

"Still, there were five...five people, you know?!" Roxy objected.

"You'll understand someday. A strong, beautiful adventurer like me being subdued and treated like a sex toy by five of those thugs? Ah, just thinking about it is enough to get me pregnant."

"I don't want to understand."

When Roxy was at the University of Magic, she was still a child and didn't understand the appeal of having a lover or being married. The first time she ever thought about wanting something like that was when she saw how intimate Paul and Zenith were with each other. That was when she finally decided she wanted the same for herself.

Still, how? She'd wondered at the time. Then she remembered what an acquaintance at the university told her. That acquaintance had met her husband in the depths of a maze. Their shared struggle and the way they overcame it led to their marriage.

This is it, Roxy thought. *If I dive into a labyrinth, I should be able to find a partner, too.*

That fantasy grew larger and larger inside her head. She would somehow bump into someone who was tall, manly, and fashionably dressed—a young human man with a youthful appeal—in the depths of a labyrinth, and he would save her. Then the two of them would combine their strengths to make their escape, and in so doing, their love would bud and blossom. The youth would discover one of his friends had died, and Roxy would comfort him. That would be their first night together.

When she actually did journey into a labyrinth, those fantasies were quickly shattered. A labyrinth was a harsh place, and the adventurers who entered them were a stern lot. The only youthful-looking person among them was Roxy herself.

By the fifth floor there were no other solo adventurers. By the tenth floor she decided things were tough enough that she needed to gather a party, but people mocked her for her childlike appearance and laughed her off countless times. She got stubborn after that and continued further downwards on foot. Ah, the stupidity of youth. She came close to death numerous times, but was lucky enough to escape its clutches. She never wanted to repeat that again.

"Well, you have to start by finding your first man, anyway. How about it? Next time, we can both—"

"Absolutely not."

The dream was shattered. Still, she held on to one hope. Perhaps it was impossible for her to find some hunk at the bottom of a labyrinth, but she could still fall in love the ordinary way and have an ordinary wedding. In the meantime, she had absolutely no intention of giving her body over to a man whose name she didn't know just because Elinalise managed to reel him in.

"Besides, I don't have the time for all of that." At least, Roxy decided she was best off alone while she was wandering the Demon Continent.

That was how Roxy made her first misstep and began her adventure across the Demon Continent.

CHAPTER 4
The Sage on Board

THAT NIGHT, the man associated with the smuggling organization, Gallus, left after telling us he would be in touch. We were forced to wait fifteen days until he sent a man with more details about the job.

The smuggled goods would be temporarily housed in a building which we would infiltrate. We would free those who had been taken and escort them back to their homes. As for how we would go about it, Gallus left that up to us.

The information was vague and the plan sounded sloppy. Still, we were just swords for hire. All we needed to do was fulfill our mission. There was some danger involved, so we decided that only Ruijerd and I would be carrying out this mission. Eris would stay behind at the inn.

It was midnight on the day of the operation. The moon was nowhere to be seen. The place in question was a pier located on the edge of the harbor. It was eerily quiet, the only sound being the echo of the ocean's waves. A suspicious figure stood by a small boat, a hood lowered over their head to hide their eyes.

If you wanted someone smuggled across the border, this was the guy. Just as we had arranged in our briefing beforehand, I handed Ruijerd over to him. Per instructions, Ruijerd's hands were shackled behind him.

A smuggler treated anyone they handled like a slave. The transport of slaves cost five green ore coins across the board, but we were exempt. The fact that Gallus had paid for us in advance didn't change how we were being handled, though. We weren't being treated as mercenaries whom Gallus had hired, but rather criminals who were smuggling slaves.

"All right then, I leave it in your hands."

The smuggler didn't say a word. He just nodded, guided Ruijerd onto the small boat, and slipped a sack over Ruijerd's head. The boat had a single boatman, but there were many others on board with sacks over their heads. Judging by their heights, none of them were children.

Once Ruijerd was safely on board, the smuggler gave the boatman a signal. The latter, who was sitting at the head of their small vessel, chanted a spell. The little boat took off without a sound, gliding across the water through the pitch black of night. I couldn't hear the words clearly, but it seemed to be a water spell that created a current to propel them forward. Something I could also do.

The little boat moved toward a merchant ship anchored in the open sea, where the slaves were transferred over to be shipped off in the early morning. Even from his spot on the smaller boat, Ruijerd continued to look my way the entire time. He knew exactly where I was, despite the bag on his head.

Watching him, I heard "Goodbye, My Lover" playing in the background of my mind. No, wait, no! He wasn't my lover! And anyway, it wasn't goodbye because this was only temporary.

The next day, I sold the lizard we had been riding around on for the past year. The steed had carried us all the way here from the city of Rikarisu, and it was reliable enough that I wished I could have taken it to the Fittoa Region with us, but it would have cost us extra to bring it on the boat. Plus, we could use horses on the Millis Continent. The horses of this world were fast, and their stamina was on an entirely different level. We didn't need to ride the lizard anymore.

Eris wrapped her arms around the lizard's neck and gave it a few pats. They exchanged no words, but it was a sad parting. The lizard had grown attached to Eris. Often, during our travels, it would lick her head all over and leave her hair drenched in drool.

We couldn't keep calling it "lizard" forever. We should at least give it a name. *Okay, from now on your name will be Guella Ha*, I decided. Guella Ha, a man of the sea who longed for more human companions.

"This one's really obedient. You must have trained it well on your travels, eh?" The merchant who handled lizards was impressed.

"I suppose so."

Ruijerd was the one who'd trained it. Not that he did anything special, but there was certainly a master-servant dynamic between him and Guella Ha. The lizard must have realized he was the most powerful person in our party. On the other hand, it didn't take a liking to me at all and bit me several times.

Hm...yeah, thinking about it just pissed me off.

"Ha ha, just what I'd expect from Dead End's Kennel Master. That'll add a little something extra to this one. Most people treat these guys too rough, and it makes my job of retraining them that much harder." The merchant was of the Rugonia tribe, a race of men with lizard heads. On the Demon Continent, the lizard men trained the lizards.

"It's only natural to treat your companions with kindness when you're traveling together."

Again, the song "Goodbye My Lover" played in my head. In my hand, I held the money we got for selling our companion off. It felt like dirty money when I thought about it that way. How strange.

Let's quit it with the name after all. It just makes me feel attached, I decided. *Goodbye then, unnamed lizard. I'll never forget how it felt to ride on you.*

"Wah..." I heard Eris sniffling.

After selling our steed, we traveled on foot to board our ship.

"Rudeus! It's a ship! It's sooo huge! Whoa! It's rocking! What is this?!" From the moment she got on board, Eris started yelling in excitement. Perhaps she had already forgotten about the lizard. Her ability to recover quickly was one of her strengths.

The ship had sails and was made of wood. It was a brand-new model that had been completed just a year ago. Not only was this its maiden voyage, but it was also pushing the envelope by traveling all the way to Zant Port.

"But this is one is a little different than the one we saw before, right?"

"You've seen a ship before, Eris?" Hadn't she said this was the first time she'd even seen the ocean?

"What are you talking about? You had one of these in your room, remember?"

Oh right, I did remember making one of these. That was a fond memory. Back then, I'd wanted to work on my earth magic, so I started crafting things. Once I realized I might be able to sell them, I started making 1/10 scale Roxy figures. I hadn't done that in a while, though. Right now, we didn't know when I would need to use my mana, so I hadn't done any training that would consume that precious resource. The only training I'd done was the physical kind, alongside Ruijerd and Eris. I really had been slacking off recently. Once things calmed down, I'd probably need to sharpen my skills again.

"I made those using my imagination, so it's no surprise that it wasn't a perfect replica," I said. Not to mention that this was supposed to be a new type of ship. As to what part of it was new, I had no idea.

"It's amazing, isn't it? That something this big can cross the ocean." Eris was incredibly impressed.

We left port three days later.

As we were on board, I began to think. A ship...a ship was a treasure trove. Now that we were on board, there had to be an event scene. I had played enough dating sims that I could say that without a shadow of a doubt.

For instance, dolphins might skip alongside the ship. The heroine would see that and say, "Look! Amazing!" And in response I would say, "My techniques in bed are even more amazing." Then she would say, "How wonderful! Make me yours!" And I would tell her, "Come on, baby, we can't do something like that right here."

Yeah, no, that wasn't quite it... Ah! That's it! When you think of a ship, you think of being attacked at sea! An octopus, a squid, a serpent, pirates, or a ghost ship, something like that. One of those would attack and sink us. We would be set adrift, then become stranded. We would arrive on a deserted island, where the heroine and I, just the two of us, would begin our lives together. At first, she would hate me, but after overcoming numerous hurdles, she would gradually grow less *tsun* and more *dere*.

Plus, there was only one thing for a man and a woman stranded on a deserted island to do together. The exchange of looks, the feverish heat... Two hot-blooded youths, breaking out in a sweat amidst the echo of crashing sea waves. Afterward, we would enjoy the sunrise together. A paradise just for the two of us.

On the issue of an octopus attack, the heroine's fate was already sealed. She would be assailed by numerous tentacles, more than you would think an eight-legged octopus could possess, and it would string her up in the air. Her body would writhe as if in agony. The creature would wrap its tentacles around her and dive beneath her clothes. It was the greatest spectacle of all, one that would make sweat pool in the palms of your hands. A sight you couldn't pull your eyes away from, even for a second.

Reality, however, was cruel.

Eris sat pale-faced in the cabin with a bucket in front of her. Her excitement over her first voyage on a ship quickly turned to nausea about midway through. I wondered why she was fine riding atop of a lizard but somehow couldn't stomach a ship.

As someone who had never experienced motion sickness, I couldn't comprehend it. Although there was one thing I could say. No matter how mild the rocking of the ship was, it did not seem to ease the suffering of a person who got seasick.

On the fourth day, an octopus showed up. At least, that's what I assumed it was. It was a startling sea-blue color and extremely large. Unfortunately, it didn't manage to capture any girls. Instead it was abruptly dispatched by an S-ranked party of bodyguards.

There shouldn't have been any escort missions available. If there had been, I would have snapped it right up. I asked a merchant nearby, who informed me that these people specialized in escorting ships. Their party name was Aqua Road. They apparently had an exclusive contract with the Shipwrights' Guild, and their primary work was acting as sea escorts. As a result, they specialized in dispatching any of the creatures that might appear on our route.

There would be no thrilling tentacle event scene after all. Too bad.

That said, there was something to glean from this. I stood aside and watched them fight, just in case something happened, so I saw the way they fought as a party.

To be honest, I snorted in laughter when I first saw their individual strengths. The swordsperson fighting in their vanguard was strong, but not as strong as Ghislaine. The one who primarily deflected the enemy's attacks and drew its attention was also a strong warrior, but nothing like Ruijerd. Their rearguard was the one who stopped the octopus, a magician who was surely weaker than I was.

I was disappointed. Was this really what an S-ranked group looked like? I thought most of the people in this world were pretty strong, but these people weren't as impressive as I'd imagined.

However, I quickly came to a different conclusion. They were an S-ranked *party*. I shouldn't have been looking at their individual strengths, but rather how they worked as a team. Even though they weren't that strong, they still managed to defeat that huge octopus. Even though they weren't that strong, they still obtained an S ranking. That was what was important. Each person fulfilled their role within the party, and that's how they wielded such power as a group. That was what teamwork meant. That was what Dead End lacked.

Each member of Dead End was powerful. But what about our teamwork? Ruijerd's teamwork was outstanding, possibly because he had operated in a squadron himself. He was skilled at group battles. Even if Eris or I made a mistake, he could cover for us. He was also great at drawing aggro, keeping the beast's eyes glued to him the entire time.

Ruijerd was also *too* strong. In truth, he could slay our opponents on his own, but we were forcing him to work with a team during battle. I wouldn't exactly call it bad, but there was no doubt that it distorted things. I thought I knew what it meant to battle as a team, but that was just in theory. Knowing the theory didn't mean you'd be able to put it into practice. I had a habit of focusing on enemies that were coming toward me, and when they outnumbered us significantly, I relied too greatly on Ruijerd.

Eris was horrible. She would listen to directives just fine, but when it came to actual battle, she couldn't match her rhythm to ours. She was too fixated on the enemy in front of her, and she threw herself too intensely into battle. The longer a fight went on, the less she would listen. Even though we called out to her, she would never cover for either of us, not even once.

Granted, neither Ruijerd nor I really needed it in the first place. Still, if this kept up and Ruijerd left us for whatever reason, I wasn't confident I could fully cover for her. Even though I had a demon eye, I still only had two hands. Just one hand for protecting myself and one hand for protecting Eris. The range of one hand was indeed limited.

"Rudeuuus..."

As I was busy with my thoughts, Eris' pale, sickly face appeared on deck. She drifted, staggering over to the edge of the ship, and vomited over the side. At this point it seemed there was nothing left in her stomach except bile.

"What are you doing up here...when I'm suffering like this..."

"Sorry. The sea is just so beautiful."

"You're so mean... Waah..." Tears pooled in her eyes as she threw her arms around me.

Her seasickness was severe.

Day five. Eris was in the cabin and down for the count as always, and I was constantly attending to her.

"U-urgh...my head hurts... Heal me...."

"Okay, okay."

I found out from one of the sailors that a little bit of healing magic could ease her suffering. Seasickness was caused by an imbalance in the autonomic nervous system. Casting a healing spell on her head would bring some temporary relief.

At least, that's how it should have worked. I couldn't continually cast it, and healing magic didn't erase all of the nausea.

"Hey...am I going...to die?"

"I'll laugh at you if you die of seasickness."

"Don't..."

There was no one else in the cabin. The ship itself was gigantic, but there weren't many people traveling from the Demon Continent to the Millis Continent. I wasn't sure if this was because the fees for passage were so much more expensive for demons than they were for humans, or because demons just found it easier living on the Demon Continent.

Eris and I were alone together.

In this quiet, dimly lit room, there she was without the power to fight back. And there I was beside her, having spent the past five days watching her weaken.

At first there was no problem with that. Except healing. That was a problem. To heal her, I needed to touch her head. Since I needed to cast my spell fairly regularly, she was using my lap as a pillow while I kept my hands wrapped around her head, repeatedly healing her.

That's when I started to feel strange. No, strange was a misleading word to use. To put it bluntly, I was starting to get horny.

Just hear me out here. There we were in a cabin and Eris, who was usually so strong-willed, was suddenly misty-eyed, her breathing erratic as she called out to me in a weak voice, entreating me. "Please, I'm begging you please, just do it (heal me)."

My internal volume controls drowned out the word *heal*. It just sounded like she was begging for it. Of course, that wasn't true. Eris was just weak. I had never experienced seasickness, but I knew it had to be awful.

There was nothing inherently sexual about touching another person. Still, she was of age, and I could feel the heat of her body. That alone was stimulating, even if the touch wasn't sexual in nature. The excitement it produced was slight, but continuously doing this for a while would spell trouble for me.

Touching, no matter where on her body, was still touching. Touching meant that we were close. Being close meant that her body was in full view. Her forehead, broken out in a cold sweat, the nape of her neck, her chest, everything.

Eris was so weak and listless. Normally, she would punch me if I touched her without reason. Right now, she was like a fish on the chopping board. That meant she was basically mine for the taking, right?

Those horrible feelings started to take root within me. I was sure she wouldn't resist me, even if I ripped off my clothes and launched myself at her. No, she *couldn't* resist me. The mere thought made my crotch feel like Excalibur before Arthur took hold of it. And in my head Arthur screamed. He was yelling at me, telling me that right now Eris couldn't resist. He told me I would never get another chance like this. Now was my chance to lose the virginity that I had been holding on to for so long.

My inner Merlin, however, urged me to resist. I had already made a decision when I promised to wait until I was fifteen. I said I would wait until this journey was over. I supported what Merlin was saying, but my ability to resist was reaching its limits.

What if I tested things out by just touching her breasts? I was sure they would be soft. And soft wasn't the only thing they would be. That's right—breasts were more than just soft. There was a firmness in the middle of all of that softness. A grail. The holy grail that my inner Arthur sought. What would happen if my hand, my Gawain, found that grail? The Battle of Camlann.

Ahh, of course, it wasn't just the holy grail. Eris' body was changing day by day, particularly her bosom. She was in the midst of puberty. I wasn't sure if it was genetic, but she was rapidly developing in a way that resembled her mother. If it kept up at this rate, she would grow into a voluptuous beauty.

Some men out there might say, "Eh, I think the smaller ones are just right." Everyone had their preferences, but I could say I'd been there at the moment when you would describe a woman's breasts as being "just right." I could take her breasts into my hands at this very moment, while they were still small.

Her breathing was erratic. "R-Rudeus...?" She looked up at me anxiously. "Are you okay?"

Her voice struck me. A voice that was usually so loud and forceful. This time it was the perfect pitch, enough to make my chest tingle.

"Uh...yeah, I'm fine, I promise. Don't worry."

"If you're suffering, you don't have to force yourself, you know?"

I don't have to force myself? So in other words, I didn't have to deny myself? Did that mean I could do whatever I wanted?

...Just kidding. I understood what she meant. She was worried about whether my mana would hold, since I was continuously healing her. I knew that already; knew that she trusted me. Trusted that I would never use this opportunity to lay a hand on her. I wouldn't betray that trust. Rudeus Greyrat would not betray that trust. That was the proper way to respond to a person's trust.

Okay, I told myself, *let's just act like a machine.* A machine. I was a healing machine. I would become a robot with no blood or tears. I would see nothing, because if I saw her face, I would do something impulsive. With that thought in mind, I decided to close my eyes. I wouldn't hear anything, either. If I heard her voice, I'd do something reckless. So I blocked off my hearing, too.

I was a silent, anti-social outcast. And since I held no earthly desires, I could do nothing impulsive. With that in mind, I closed my heart off. However, I could still feel the heat from her head and smell the scent of her body. Between those two things, my will was instantly shattered. It felt like my head was going to boil over.

Ah, I can't do this. I'm at my wits' end, I thought.

"Eris, I need to go to the bathroom."

"Oh, so that's what you were holding in. Okay... See you in a bit."

She fell for that easily. I gave her a sidelong glance before exiting the cabin. I moved quickly. I needed somewhere deserted, and I found a spot quickly enough. There I had a moment of supreme bliss.

"Phew..."

Just like that, I felt like a boy who had transformed into a sage. When I closed my eyes the sense became stronger, as if I'd reached sainthood, like a magical girl transforming and obtaining even greater powers.

"Okay, I'm back."

"Yeah, welcome back..."

I returned to the cabin with a look of enlightenment on my face, like Bodhisattva, and became a healing machine at last.

Eris returned to her normal lively self the moment we got off the boat. "I never want to ride on another ship again!"

"Yeah, but we'll have to do it one last time in order to get from Millis Continent to the Central Continent."

She looked disheartened at that, then anxious as she recalled what had transpired on the ship. "H-hey. When that happens, will you heal me the entire time again?"

"Sure, but next time I might do something naughty to you," I said matter-of-factly.

"Ugh...why would you say something so cruel?!"

It wasn't cruelty. I was the one suffering. I understood now how a dog felt, having a delicious meal set before it only to be forcefully restrained from taking a bite. There you were, your stomach completely empty with the food calling out to you, begging you to devour it, and you couldn't. You could gulp down as much water as you wanted to try and temporarily satisfy the ache in your belly, but it was a futile effort. The meal wouldn't disappear, and your stomach would feel empty again soon enough.

"You're really cute, Eris. I'm desperately trying to resist the temptation to do anything to you."

"F-fine, I guess if that's how it has to be. Next time you can touch me, but only a little bit, okay?" Her face was bright tomato red. It really was adorable. However, there was far too great of a gap between the enormity of my desire and the "little" that she offered.

"Unfortunately, 'just a little' isn't going to cut it. Please, let's wait until you're ready for me to dive in and have my way with you."

Eris was speechless. I didn't want her to fuel my expectations. I wanted her to let me keep that promise I made to her. If I broke it and put my hands on her, we would both be upset about it afterward.

"Anyway, let's get going."

"O-okay. Sure." Eris recovered quickly and was soon in high spirits as we started walking toward the town.

The townscape before us was not much different than Wind Port. But this was Zant Port, a city at the northern edge of the Millis Continent. Millis Continent. We were finally here, yet we still had a long way to go.

"Rudeus, what's wrong?"

"No, it's nothing."

Best to forget about how long our journey would be. The important thing right now was setting out for the next city.

Before we did that, however, we needed to get some money and buy a horse. And before that, we had to finish our current job. Now that we had come this far, it was time to see this mission to completion. That said, our job didn't start until nightfall. We still had some time before then. So, what to do?

We had already exchanged our money on the Demon Continent, so there was no need to visit the Adventurers' Guild. I decided we would get ourselves an inn. That way we could recover from our tiring journey on the ship. Our job came later. Ruijerd would have to suffer in his uncomfortable living conditions a little while longer, but...well, he would just have to endure.

And that was how we arrived on the Millis Continent.

CHAPTER 5
The Demon in the Warehouse

T HE LAYOUT of the city of Zant Port was similar to that of Wind Port. There were a number of rolling hills at its edge, and a harbor that was livelier than the city itself. The Adventurers' Guild was similarly closer to the harbor than it was to the city's center.

That said, there were some contrasts. There were noticeably far more wooden buildings here than there had been in Wind Port. They were also painted in riots of color, perhaps to protect the material from the salty sea air. Trees lined the road, and one could see a forest beyond the city's edge.

Green was everywhere. It was a sharp contrast to the Demon Continent, which had been all whites, grays and browns. An ocean was all that separated the two continents and yet they were like different worlds.

I should have expected as much since this was the Millis Continent, but the people roaming the streets were not the outlandish mix of different demon tribes I had seen before. Instead there were beastfolk, elves, dwarves, and hobbits—races of people that all closely resembled humans.

Before we went to find ourselves an inn, I had to check the state of our finances. In the Demon Continent's currency, we had two green ore coins, eighteen steel iron coins, five scrap iron coins, and three stone coins. That was it. When we exchanged it, we received three Millis gold coins, seven Millis large copper coins, and two Millis copper coins. Less than I assumed we would have, but I suspected that was because of transaction fees. If we'd used an exchange business that hadn't been licensed with the guild, they would have surely taken more. This was still within an acceptable range.

"We should stay in an inn close to the guild, right?"

"Yeah, we need to take on some missions," Eris agreed.

That depended on how things went down tonight. Assuming it went smoothly, we would be working on jobs from the guild while simultaneously spreading the good name of Dead End. So far, it seemed the name wasn't widely known here in Millis Continent. The day that name lost all its dire associations might soon be upon us.

With that in mind, we began searching for an inn close to the guild. Mysteriously enough, all of the conveniently priced ones had no rooms left. This was the first time I'd experienced this. Sure, we had been turned away before because an inn was full, but I never dreamed that almost all of them would be that way.

Was there some kind of festival or something going on? When I asked, one of the inn proprietors replied, "The rainy season is almost upon us. Almost all the good inns are going to be fully booked."

The rainy season was a weather phenomenon peculiar to the Great Forest, a continuous rainfall that lasted three whole months. The deluge made the Great Forest, as well as the highway, impassable. There were many guests who booked long stays at the inns as a result.

Most people would usually avoid getting stuck in a place like this during the rainy season, but apparently certain monsters only appeared during this time, thanks to the rains that washed them toward the city. The materials harvested from those monsters sold for a lot of coin, so many adventurers came to town and stayed during this season.

When I heard that, I decided to change my plans. If we spent the next three months diligently raking in cash here, we could earn all our expenses for the rest of the journey. We could also spread good word of Ruijerd's name at the same time. Deciding on a plan of action would make the rest of our trip on the Millis Continent smooth and relaxing.

That said, don't count your chickens before they some-thing-or-other, right? We didn't have much cash, and we couldn't find an inn to stay at, either. The only places with open rooms were either far above our budget, or exceedingly shitty.

You couldn't pay with money you didn't have, so we were left with only one option: to take residence in an unsavory lot and stay at what was, frankly, a slum lodge. One night was three large copper coins and there were no other services offered, including meals. At least it was cheap, and decent if we were only using it for sleeping. We had stayed in far worse places in the Demon Continent. Though it might be worth moving somewhere else once we managed to save up some coin.

"Hmm, I guess it's not too bad!" Eris was a daughter of a noble family, but she had no qualms about the dilapidated state of the building or its lack of services.

In fact, I was the one who had complaints. "I personally would like more pleasant accommodations."

"You're acting like a big baby."

As much as I wanted to reply with, "Oh yeah? Well you're one to talk", I couldn't. With careful recollection, I remembered that this young, "noble" girl used to sleep soundly on a bale of hay in a roach-infested stable that reeked of horse dung. She wasn't like me. I still longed for the warmth of a nice bed even after being reincarnated.

I decided not to "act like a big baby". All I could do was use magic to create a hot wind that would annihilate any dust mites, then quickly clean the room. I wasn't necessarily a clean freak. Honestly, I actually liked things to be a little messy, but sometimes in inns like these the people who stayed before us forgot some of their things. There might be some coin left underneath the bed, or a small ring that had fallen off a cabinet. We could pocket any money we found, but sometimes if there was a ring or something similar left behind, there might be a request for it at the guild. It might give us a cash reward, regardless of the request's rank. Typically this was small change, but sometimes it could fetch you a hefty sum. That was why I carefully cleaned the room.

In the meantime, Eris borrowed a buck to do some simple laundry. Then she quickly performed routine care on her equipment. By the time we were both finished, the sun was beginning to set.

"Eris, it's about time for us to go pick up Ruijerd." I immediately remembered where our inn was located. The slums were close, which meant public safety wasn't a guarantee.

We'd once stayed in an inn close to the slums. A burglar broke into our room while we were out on a job. Ruijerd had followed the crook's tracks and punished them severely, but the goods they stole from us had already been passed off to someone else and we never got them back. The articles weren't particularly important to us at the time.

Thus, I had no plans to leave anything precious in this hotel room while we were out. Still, it seemed prudent to put in some crime prevention measures. It also gave me a good pretext not to bring Eris along with me.

"Eris, you stay here and keep an eye on our luggage."

"You're leaving me here? I can't go with you?"

"It's not like that, it's just that this isn't really a safe area around here."

"That's fine; it's not like any of this stuff is particularly important."

I was shocked. Eris didn't realize the importance of crime prevention. We would be in trouble if we had our daily commodities stolen, since we didn't have the money to replace them. I had to use this opportunity to instill in her the importance of guarding herself against would-be thieves.

"Don't you understand? Someone might steal the underwear you just washed."

"The only person who would steal something like that is you!"

I groaned inwardly at that burn.

...But you know, Eris, I never tried to steal your underwear *after* you'd washed them. Not even once.

I walked through the city at night, alone. Eris took quite some time to persuade. Crime prevention really was important, though.

We were instructed to carry out our job at night, but our employer never specified the hour. Any time after the sun set was fine as long as we rescued the captives. We were free to operate on our own time. However, with the rainy season almost upon us, the smugglers would be eager to move their ship as quickly as possible, so we couldn't dawdle.

At presently, Ruijerd was being treated as a slave. They would do the bare minimum to keep him alive, but he might have endured harsh treatment this past week. They surely hadn't fed him anything decent. He was probably hungry. And when people got hungry, they got angry. That was why I had to hurry.

With Ruijerd's spear in one hand, I made my way to the wharf, and then to the pier on the edge. There stood four large wooden warehouses. I slipped inside the one labelled "Warehouse Three".

Inside was a single man, quietly cleaning. He had one of the most common hairstyles at the turn of the century, a mohawk. I went up to him and asked, "Yo, Steve. How's Jane, you know, the one that lives by the beach?" That was our password.

Mohawk gave me a quizzical look. "Hey kid, what are you doing here?"

Oh crap, had I gotten it wrong? No, that wasn't it—maybe he just didn't believe me because I was a kid.

"I'm on an errand for my master. I'm here to pick up some cargo."

The man seemed to understand once I said that. He nodded quietly and said, "Follow me." Then he headed deeper into the warehouse.

I followed him in silence. Deep within the warehouse was a wooden box large enough to fit maybe five people inside. Mohawk drew a torch from within and the box moved. A set of stairs appeared below it, and Mohawk motioned his chin toward them as if telling me to descend.

When I did so, I realized we were in a damp cave. Mohawk came behind me with his lit torch and proceeded ahead. I followed after him, careful of where I placed my feet so that I wouldn't slip.

We continued walking for almost an hour. Finally, we left the cave and found ourselves in the middle of the forest. Apparently we were outside the city now. We continued to walk until we came across a large building hidden among rows of trees. It didn't look at all like a warehouse, but rather a rich man's villa.

So this was their holding area.

"I'm sure you already know this, but you better keep this place a secret. If you don't..."

"Yes, I know." I gave a firm nod. If I told anyone, they would hunt me down and kill me, right? Gallus had already told me that back in Wind Port. They would have been better off making me sign in blood rather than with a promise made of empty words. So why didn't they? Because there were races that didn't have fingerprints. Also, it was likely no one wanted to commit something like that to writing. It would only leave evidence of their wrongdoing.

"..."

Mohawk knocked on the front door. *Bang, bang. Bang, bang.* There must have been a rule for how to knock as well.

After a while a white-haired man in a butler's uniform appeared from within. He checked both of our faces before curtly saying, "Enter."

Enter we did. In front of us, a set of stairs led to the second floor. On either side was another set that led to the basement. There were doors both to our right and left. Frankly speaking, it looked like a mansion's lobby area. In one corner, some shady-looking men had their elbows crooked on a round table.

I started feeling nervous.

That's when the white-haired butler looked at me, suspicion in his eyes as he asked, "And who referred you?"

"Ditz." That was the name Gallus told us to say.

"Him, huh? Still, I wouldn't have expected him to use a child for this. He sure is a cautious one."

"Such is the nature of the goods we're handling."

"Hm, indeed. Take it quickly then. It's terrifying and beyond our power." The butler produced a ring of keys from his breast pocket and passed one over to Mohawk. "Room 202."

Mohawk nodded quietly and we started walking.

I could hear the squeak of the floor beneath his feet, as well as the sound of someone moaning somewhere within the building. The smell of an animal occasionally wafted by. That's when I noticed there was a room adjacent to the main area with iron bars across it. I peeked inside. In the faint light that filtered in, I could see a magical circle on the floor. Contained within its bounds was a large beast that was chained down and sprawled out. It was too dark to be certain, but I had never seen that kind of creature on the Demon Continent before. It must have been something native to the Millis Continent.

Where were these slaves who had been taken captive? We were told to free them, but we weren't told where they were located. Perhaps Ruijerd would know.

Mohawk descended stairs located deeper within the mansion. The butler had said Room 202, so I assumed that would be upstairs, but it seemed it was in the basement instead.

"So it's located underground, huh?"

"The second floor is a dummy to fake people out."

So that meant the items on the second floor were of no concern should someone find them. Goods that were highly taxed or would otherwise earn a harsh sentence if smuggled were kept downstairs.

"This is it." Mohawk stopped in front of a door with a plate that read "202". When I peeked inside, I saw Ruijerd with his hands cuffed behind his back, emerald sprigs of hair beginning to crop up on his head. It was no surprise that after leaving him like this for a week, he now looked like he had moss growing on the top of his head.

"Thank you for your help."

Mohawk nodded and took his post outside the front door. A lookout, I assumed. "Don't remove his shackles here. There's nothing we can do to stop a Superd if it goes out of control here." Mohawk looked a little pale as he said that.

It seemed the emerald-colored hair, as little as there was on Ruijerd's head, was effective. Mohawk would be even more terrified if I removed Ruijerd's binds and started commanding him. Nah, there was no need to put on an act like that—pretending to be the weak evil genius who controlled the monster.

Now where did I put that key for his shackles? I searched my breast pocket, but it was nowhere to be found. Perhaps I left it back at the inn. It was too much of a bother to worry about, so I decided to just use my magic. As I stepped closer to Ruijerd, I noticed a grim look on his face.

Yep, I knew it. People get pissed off when they're hungry, I thought. *Just wait a little longer and we'll get you some food to—*

"Rudeus, bring your ear close," Ruijerd whispered.

"What is it?"

When I pressed my face in closer, Mohawk seemed to panic and said, "H-hey! Stop that! He'll bite it off!"

Nah, don't worry. It's Ruijerd we're talking about, he'll let me off with a play bite, I thought as I leaned closer.

"They've kidnapped children. Seven of them."

Oh? More than I would have expected.

"Beastfolk children. Taken against their will. I can hear them crying even from here."

"Hm, maybe they're the ones we're supposed to rescue?"

"Don't know. But there doesn't seem to be anyone else here."

Children. Slaves, I assumed. Amongst whom was the person Gallus said would cause them trouble in the future. Or perhaps it was someone else, someone important.

"We're going to save them, of course. Right?"

"Well, that is the job we took on, after all," I replied.

Either way, we could check each room to be sure. There was just one problem remaining.

"There's quite a few bodyguards throughout this building."

"I know that," he said.

"So what are we going to do about them?"

Even though it was Ruijerd we were talking about, it would still be difficult for him to go undetected and release all of those slaves.

"Kill them all."

Scary!

"Kill them all, huh...?"

"They kidnapped children." He had a look of disbelief on his face. As if I had betrayed him.

It wasn't as if I'd expressed opposition. Gallus never specified what methods we could and couldn't use. Judging by the way he talked, he probably assumed I would let Ruijerd massacre them all. But I'd originally planned to release him and leave, then stealthily infiltrate and free the captives. It seemed my plans had been too naive. Killing them all might not reflect honorably on the name of Ruijerd's tribe, at least in my opinion, but we had no choice this time.

"Just don't leave a single one alive."

I didn't say that to be ruthless or cruel. A smuggling organization would repay a customer who had betrayed them by sending assassins they'd reared since birth. The only thing that awaited traitors was a merciless death.

I wasn't sure what Gallus would do after this. He might send assassins after us to keep our mouths shut. As long as Ruijerd was with us, we had no fear of assassins, but we wouldn't be able to sleep in peace. There was also no guarantee that Ruijerd would be with us all the time.

"Yeah, leave it to me."

Woot woot, just the response I would have expected, Ruijerd! Those were comforting words.

"I won't leave anyone alive. Not a single one."

Scary. A blue vein bulged in his forehead. Lately I thought he'd mellowed out a bit, but today he was blood-thirsty. Just what had these smugglers done to piss him off this much?

"Can I ask what they did to those kids?"

"You'll know when you see them."

That didn't really tell me anything.

"Don't worry. You don't have to get your hands dirty," Ruijerd said, misunderstanding my demeanor.

My body froze and I said, "No." His words were like a thorn that pricked at my heart. "I'll...do it too."

It was true that in this past year, I had avoided taking anyone's life. I killed beasts without question, even those that were humanoid. I did not, however, commit murder. Partly because I had no need to, but there were also many reasons for me not to. I had never felt the impulse to kill anyone before, either.

This world was unforgiving. It was a world where people fought life-or-death battles daily. Eventually, I would have to kill someone. That was a situation I would one day face. I thought I had mentally prepared myself for that, but what I had done wasn't mental preparation.

All I'd done was reduce the strength of my stone cannon to a level where it wasn't capable of killing anyone.

In the end, I did have qualms about taking someone's life. I could claim otherwise if I wanted, but the truth was that I didn't want to commit the taboo of murder. I hadn't prepared myself, *couldn't* prepare myself. Ruijerd sensed that. That's why he specifically said what he'd said. He was looking out for me.

"Don't make that face. Those hands of yours are for protecting Eris."

Oh well. I supposed he was right. There was no point in forcing myself to kill. I decided to leave the job to Ruijerd today. If he could do it by himself, then it was better to entrust it to him. If that made me a wuss, then fine. It was better to focus on what I was capable of doing than what I wasn't.

"All right then. I'll free the children. Do you know where they're at?"

"The next door over."

"All right then. Try to gather the dead bodies. Let's burn them all afterward."

"Understood."

Without further speaking, I removed his shackles. The door creaked as Ruijerd stood up slowly.

"Hey, you! How the heck did get your shackles off?!" Mohawk panicked.

"Don't worry. He'll listen to what I say."

"R-really?" Mohawk seemed a bit relieved to hear me say that.

I passed Ruijerd's spear over to him. "Although he'll still go berserk, anyway."

"Huh...?"

Mohawk was the first victim. Ruijerd slew him without making a noise. Then, just as silently, he ran toward the stairs. I moved in the opposite direction to the room where the children were being held.

"Gaaaaah!"

"A S-Superd! He's got his shackles off!"

"Shit! He's holding a spear!"

"It's a demon! Aaaah, it's a demon, aaah!"

The screams from downstairs started just as I reached the door.

CHAPTER 6

The Beastfolk Children

T HE ROOM was dark. Within the shadows were boys and girls with nervous looks on their faces, their bodies writhing. There were four girls and three boys, seven children in total. All of them were around my age. They were all naked, all with beast or elf ears. Their hands were bound behind them, and they all shrank from me.

What a sight it was—like a young version of Kannon, the Goddess of Mercy, a Buddhist Bodhisattva. This was Eden. No, perhaps it was heaven. Had I finally arrived in heaven? No, I still hadn't found the green baby yet!

This was no time to get excited. With only one exception, their eyes were all swollen from crying, and several had bluish-black bruises on their faces. My head cooled immediately. They were crying and screaming, so they probably got hit for being noisy.

The same thing had happened when Eris and I were kidnapped. In this world, kidnappers showed no concern for the children they took captive. Ruijerd must have heard them being mercilessly tortured from his spot in the neighboring room. That was why he couldn't hold himself back.

From a quick glance, they didn't seem to have been sexually abused. Perhaps because they were still young, or perhaps because it would lower their sale value. Whatever the reason, it was the one mercy amidst this misfortune.

Normally I would look at naked girls and my eyes would go immediately to their breasts, but right now, my inner pervert had been weakened. I had just decided to become a hermit before disembarking from the ship, after all. Sadly, my new profession hadn't increased my intelligence at all.

Three of the girls were still sobbing, tears running down their cheeks. Two of the boys regarded me with terrified looks on their faces.

The third was crumpled on the floor, barely breathing. I healed him first before removing the shackles from his wrists. His mouth was gagged so tightly I couldn't get it off. With no other choice, I had to sear it off. It might have burned him a little, but I figured he could handle it. I did the same for the other two boys, healing them and taking off their wrist cuffs.

"U-um...who are...?"

The words were spoken in the Beast God tongue so I was slightly taken aback, but I could speak it, at least. "I came to save you. You three, go act as lookouts at the door. If you see anyone coming, tell me immediately."

The three of them exchanged nervous glances.

"You're men, right? You can at least do that, can't you?"

Their expressions hardened and they nodded, running off toward the door. There was no other meaning to my directions. It wasn't like I just wanted them out of the way so I could ogle the girls without interruption.

Ruijerd was causing a ruckus above, so probably no one would come this way. Still, we couldn't take any chances. Before I entered the room, I had set my demon eye to show me one second into the future, but I wouldn't be able to see anything if I didn't look behind me.

I proceeded to remove the girls' shackles. Some were more well-endowed than others, but I didn't discriminate. I admired them equally as I took off their binds. I also didn't touch them more than was necessary. I wanted them to think of the Rudeus before them as nothing short of a gentleman.

I also healed their bruises. It was my time to enjo— err, I mean *treat their wounds*. After all, you had to touch someone to heal them. So there was no other meaning behind it. Yes, one of the girls did have bruises on her chest, but I swear I had no ulterior motives.

This one had a broken rib. That couldn't be good... And this other had her femur broken. Those men really had been vicious.

The girls hid themselves with their hands as they stood up. They removed their gags themselves. Was it my imagination, or was the strong-willed girl with cat ears glaring at me?

"Thank you for...hic...saving us." The girl with dog ears thanked me as she shyly hid her body. She spoke in the Beast God tongue, of course.

"Just to make sure, you can all understand me, right?"

When they all nodded, I breathed a sigh of relief. Apparently my Beast God tongue was intelligible.

It seemed Ruijerd still wasn't done, and I couldn't lead these children through a slaughterhouse. It might cause them further trauma, so maybe I would just admire this scenery for a little bit longer...or not. I should probably ask them about what happened.

"If you don't mind me asking, why were you all brought here?"

"Mew?"

I directed my question to the cat-eared girl, the one who seemed the most headstrong. She was the only one among the seven who didn't have a fresh trail of tears down her cheeks. Instead, her body seemed to be the most battered, broken and bruised. Not quite as bad as what Eris had experienced, but her injuries were still the worst. Second worst was the first boy I helped, but unlike that boy, she still had a spark of life in her eyes.

This girl might be even more strong-willed than Eris. No, she was probably older than Eris had been back then. If they were the same age, there was no way Eris would have lost.

Okay, what the hell was I getting all competitive over?

"We were playing in the forest when a strange man suddenly grabbed us, mew!"

It was a shock to my system. Mew! Her sentence ended in "mew"! A real mew! Completely different from Eris' imitation. This girl was a real, genuine cat beastfolk. It wasn't just because she was speaking in Beast God tongue either. She definitely said "mew" at the end there. Amazing.

No. I couldn't get distracted. "So that means all of you were taken against your will?" I tried to tamp down my emotions and remain cool as I asked.

The girls all nodded. Good. If they'd been sold by struggling parents, or sold themselves because they didn't have the means to live anymore, then our efforts to free them would have been in vain. Good. We were saving people. I was really glad about that.

"It's over." Ruijerd had returned. The mossy green color was gone from his scalp, and a forehead protector was fastened around his head. His clothes were pristine. There wasn't a single drop of blood on them. I would've expected nothing less.

"Good work. Were there any other people held captive?" I asked.

"None."

"Then let's find some clothes for these guys. They'll catch a cold if we leave them like this."

"Understood," Ruijerd replied.

"Okay, guys," I told them. "Please just wait a little bit longer."

We split up and started searching for suitable clothes. We couldn't find anything for children. Their clothes must have been stripped off and discarded when their captors abducted them. But what for? I didn't understand. It was a mystery to me why they left these kids naked. Not having clothes was a serious problem. We couldn't even take them into a clothing store if they were naked.

"Hm?" I happened to glance out the window, only to see a mountain of dead bodies. Each of them bore a single stab wound, either in the heart or the throat. Seeing something like that would have terrified me long ago, but this time it was reassuring. Still, I didn't expect there to be so many of them. The smell of blood hung thick. It would lure monsters.

Let's burn these quickly, I thought, and stepped out of the building.

I stood before the odorous mountain of corpses and created a fireball. A radius of five meters seemed appropriate for this use. In fire magic, increasing the power of a spell also increased its size for some reason. I didn't want to smell the stench of burnt flesh, though, so I decided to incinerate them in a single blast.

"Whoops!"

The resulting fire was clearly too powerful, because it instantly spread to the building. I quickly turned to water magic to extinguish the flames.

That was close. I almost turned myself into a pyromaniac.

Aw crap, maybe I should have stripped them of their clothes first, I thought. They would probably reek of blood and turn my stomach, but they could still be worn after I washed them.

"Rudeus. I'm finished."

As I was preoccupied with those thoughts, Ruijerd came out of the building. The children were all with him, all clothed. By clothed, I meant they were all in feathered robes.

"Where did you find clothes like that?"

"I cut the curtains."

Oho. You are a clever one, I thought. *A true font of wisdom.*

The next objective in our mission was to return the children to their homes. That meant bringing them to the city and guiding them to their parents.

I lit the torches at the building's front entrance and made each of the children carry one. I decided to take a different route back. It would be troublesome if another smuggler found us, and that underground route was probably created to protect people from the forest's beasts. We didn't need that.

"Mew!" The cat-eared girl suddenly cried out. The noise echoed in the darkness around us.

"What's wrong?" I asked, wishing she wouldn't be so loud.

"Mew! Was there a dog in that building we just came out of?!" She clung to Ruijerd's leg. There was a clear look of desperation on her face.

"There was."

"Why didn't you rescue it?!"

That's right, there was a dog. Wait, that was a dog? It was freakin' huge.

"You guys came first."

Their reproachful eyes fixed upon Ruijerd.

Oh, come on, I thought. *We just saved you guys. There's no reason for you to give us that look.* "Just so you know, he's the one who saved you."

"W-well, I'm grateful for that, mew. But..."

"If you're grateful, then you should say thank you."

When I said that, they all bowed their heads to him. *Good*, I thought. *You should all be more grateful.*

This might have been a mission we were given by a smuggler from the organization that kidnapped them in the first place, but it was also true that Ruijerd was genuinely concerned about them. Though it was also true we were demanding their gratitude when they'd never asked us to save them.

"I'll go back and free the dog. Ruijerd, you take these guys to the city."

"Understood. Where should we go once we get there?"

"Wait just outside the city," I instructed. I retraced my steps.

Where were we supposed to take them after this? That was a difficult question. At first, I considered bringing them to the Adventurers' Guild. Then we could put out a request saying, "We have children in our custody; please search for their parents," and entrust the kids to the guild. That would be the end of it.

However, Gallus said himself that the smuggling organization wasn't a single group. If we moved too openly, we would be discovered. Considering our conversations, Gallus wouldn't be able to help us if that happened. Our involvement was better left undiscovered. For our sake as well as his.

In that case...what if we left the kids with the city garrison and fled the city as quickly as possible? No, if the kids talked, our identities would be discovered. Then the smuggling organization would find out. Plus the rainy season was almost upon us. If we left the city, we had nowhere else to go. We might even be mistaken for kidnappers ourselves.

Hmm. This was troubling. Perhaps I hadn't considered this thoroughly enough. I had been sure we could free them, but I'd put too little thought into what came after that. Maybe we should pin the blame for the attack on someone else? Yeah, maybe that was a good idea. If I wrote "The Demon World's Great Emperor Kishirika was here" on the wall, they might actually believe it. Kishirika did say to rely on her if I needed anything, after all.

"Welp." I'd arrived back at the building, still undecided on a course of action.

I found the room where I previously saw the magic circle. When I entered, the beast greeted me with a suspicious look in its eyes. It didn't wag its tail, and it didn't bark. It was lethargic.

"It's definitely a dog."

It was a puppy chained within that magic circle. You could tell it was a puppy at a glance, but it was enormous. It was about two meters tall. Why were all the dogs and cats of this world so big?

Its fur had appeared white when I first looked at it, but on closer inspection, it was actually silver. It seemed to glitter, but that was probably due to the lighting. A large silver baby Shiba Inu, with a refined, intelligent look on its face.

"I'm going to help you—ooouch!"

The moment I tried to enter the magic circle, it repelled me. Not quite like a zap. The sensation was difficult to explain, but it was like the pain receptors in my brain were being triggered. It seemed this magic circle was actually a barrier. A barrier was a type of healing magic—a construction I knew nothing about.

"Hmm." I studied the borders of the magic circle. It emitted a bluish-white light, faintly illuminating the room. The light coming from it meant that mana was circulating. If I could cut off the source of its fuel, the circle would disappear. Roxy taught me that. It was the quintessential method of removing magical traps.

The fuel source... In other words, a magic crystal.

Yet as far as I could see, there was no such crystal to be found. No... that just meant I hadn't found it *yet*. Where had they hidden it? Probably underground. Maybe I should use earth magic to remove the circle? Who knew what would occur if I tried to forcibly dispel a magic circle such as this?

Hm, wait, I thought. *Wait, wait, wait. Let's think about this more simply.*

How were those guys even planning to get this dog out of that circle in the first place? There hadn't been a magician amongst the corpses I'd seen. There had to be a way for a complete beginner to remove this trap.

First I considered where the magic crystal could be. I thought it had to be underground. However, if it were underground, those guys wouldn't have been able to pull it out. It had to be somewhere they could extract it. But it also had to be somewhere where it could still fuel mana into the trap.

"Hm, so above rather than below?"

I decided to check upstairs. I went to the room directly above, where I found a smaller magic circle and what appeared to be a wooden lantern. In it was what I assumed was a magic crystal.

Very good. I was lucky to be able to find it with my first guess.

I carefully lifted the lantern and the magic circle below gently dissipated. When I returned to the ground floor, I saw that the one surrounding the dog was completely gone. It seemed the upper and lower circles had been linked together after all. Nice, nice.

"Grrr...!"

The dog looked menacingly at me and snarled as I approached. For as long as I could remember, animals had never liked me. This wasn't any different.

I studied the dog's physical condition. Its growl was still a powerful thing, but it didn't have the same strength in its body. It looked exhausted. No doubt because it was hungry.

Still, those chains were suspicious. There was probably some meaning to the pattern etched upon them. Maybe I should remove them. No, that might be dangerous. If those chains were restraining its power, then the moment I released them, it might attack me. I could heal a little bite, but...

"What should I do so you don't bite me?"

When I asked that, the dog responded, "Woof?" It titled its head at me as if it understood the words.

Hm.

"If you don't bite me, I'll take that collar off of you and return you to your master. How about it?" I spoke to it in Beast God tongue, and when I did, the dog ceased its growling and quietly stretched itself out on the ground. It seemed it did understand. Being in a different world was convenient after all. You could even talk to dogs.

I tried using magic to sever the chain. It broke easily. Once it did, power instantly returned to the dog's body. It immediately stood up and tried to dash off, but I stopped it.

"Wait, wait, you still have a collar on you."

It looked at me and obediently lay down once more.

I tried my best to remove the collar, but it had no keyhole. If there was no keyhole, there was no way to unlock it. That was weird. How did they intend to ever remove it? Or did they never intend to do so? It was a tough battle, but I managed to find a joint in the collar. Apparently this was one of those collars you couldn't remove once it was snapped on.

"I'm going to take it off now, so don't move." I carefully conjured earth magic into the small juncture where the collar joined together, using magic to force it open. There was a *clang*, and finally it came off.

"There we go."

The puppy shook its neck. "Woof!"

"Whoa!"

The dog hooked its front paws on either of my shoulders, and its weight knocked me over. I fell limply to the ground, and the dog started slobbering all over my face.

"Woof!"

Aah! You can't, little puppy! I have a wife and husband…!

I tried to push the great silver ball of fur off of me, but it was too heavy and, moreover, soft and fluffy. Silky and soft. That was all well and good, but it was heavy. Its weight on my chest was enough to make my bones creak. Moving it seemed difficult. I gave up on not being licked since there was nothing I could do. Instead I focused on enjoying the feel of its fur until it grew bored of lapping at my face.

And boy was it fluffy. Or, as the kids say, "a floof".

For you to be this soft… Hey, wait. You're using some kind of fabric softener, aren't you? I thought, only for another voice in my head to reply in kind. *Aww, but I'm not using anything~*

"Bastard! What have you done to the Sacred Beast?!"

"Huh?"

Just as the ball of fur finally seemed satisfied, a voice rang out. Still sprawled on the ground, I looked up, wondering if one of those smugglers had managed to survive.

I was greeted by chocolate-colored skin, beast ears, and a tiger's tail. Ghislaine...? No, it wasn't. They looked similar, but it wasn't her. The hairy, muscular part was the same, but there was something a bit different. Ghislaine's biggest feature was absent. It was the chest—this person's was flat. This person had pecs where Ghislaine had a full bosom. It was a man.

The man put his hand to his mouth, as if he were about to shout.

Ah, crap! He's going to do something. I've got to run. But I can't move!

"Doggy, move. I need to run from this guy!"

The dog moved.

I scrambled to my feet and activated my demon eye. I could see what would happen.

The man has his hand still pressed to his mouth.

I thought he wasn't going to do anything, but then suddenly he roared. "Graaaaah!" The volume was overpowering. It was a voice many times more shrill than any

Eris had ever produced. The sound felt like it had mass. My eardrums rang, and my brain trembled.

By the time I realized what was happening, I had collapsed. I couldn't stand. This was bad. I had to heal myself, but I couldn't move my hands. What the hell was this, some kind of magic?

Crap. Crap, crap, crap. I couldn't use magic? I tried to channel my mana but...no good.

The man grabbed me by the collar and lifted me into the air. I was brought level with the frowning face of a man, his brows knitted together.

"Hm. Still just a kid. Can't bring myself to kill you."

Ah, it seemed I was safe. Thank goodness. I was glad I looked like a kid.

"Gyes, what is it?"

Another man appeared. He looked similar to Ghislaine. but had white hair. An older man.

"Father. I've subdued one of the smugglers."

"A smuggler? Isn't that a child?"

"But he was trying to attack the Sacred Beast."

"Hm."

"He had an obscene look on his face as he fondled it. Perhaps he isn't the age that he appears."

N-no, you're wrong. I'm twelve. I'm definitely not a forty-five-year-old man on the inside, I protested in my head.

"Woof!" When the beast barked, Gyes and the other man both took a knee before it.

"I apologize. We should have moved with more haste, but instead we were late in our rescue."

"Woof!"

"To think that this boy would lay his hands on your holiness... Gah...!"

"Woof!"

"What? It didn't bother you? How benevolent...!"

They seemed to be having a conversation, although the dog was only saying "woof woof" the whole time.

"Gyes, I found Tona's scent in a room in the basement. She was here. That is certain," the old man said.

Who was Tona? From the context of their conversation, I guessed it was one of the beastfolk children.

"Let's take this young boy back to the village and interrogate him. He might have taken them somewhere. And once we make him spill, we'll set out again and search—"

"There's no time. The last ship leaves tomorrow."

Gyes gritted his teeth.

"We have no choice but to give up. Consider it fortuitous enough that we managed to save the Sacred Beast."

"And what'll we do with *this*?"

"Take him home with us. He may be a child, but if he

was working with those smugglers, then he'll have to be punished."

Gyes nodded and tied my hands behind me with a rope. Then he hoisted me onto his shoulder. The dog toddled along behind him, glancing worriedly at me.

It's okay. Don't worry. These guys don't seem to be smugglers, I told myself. *They came here to rescue those kids. So if I talk to them, they'll understand. I just have to wait until they'll let me.*

"Hm..." When we stepped outside, the elder twitched his nose. "The smell lingers."

"A smell? The stench of blood is so thick I can't tell."

"It's faint, but it's the smell of Tona and the others. There's one more as well. That demon's scent."

The moment he mentioned "that demon", Gyes' expression hardened. "Are you saying that demon took Tona and the others?"

"Hard to tell. Perhaps he saved them," the old man suggested.

"No way. That can't be."

It seemed they had caught wind of Ruijerd's scent.

"Gyes. I'm going to follow the trail. You take the boy and the Sacred Beast and return to the village."

"No, I'm going with you," Gyes protested.

"You're too short-tempered. And that boy may not be one of those smugglers after all, you know?" Unsurprisingly, the elder's words had a wisdom to them.

That's right, I thought. *I'm not a smuggler, so please let me explain.*

"Even so, there's still no mistaking the fact that he touched the Sacred Beast with his filthy hands. This boy smells like an aroused human. As unbelievable as it sounds, he showed signs of sexual excitement toward the Sacred Beast."

What?!

Absolutely untrue! I thought. *I do not have any sexual interest in dogs! Young girls, however... No! That's not a good defense, either!*

"In that case, throw him in a cell. But do not put your hands on him until I return home."

"Yes, sir!"

The older man gave a nod before running off into the darkness of the forest.

As Gyes watched him go, he said to me, "Hmph, he just saved your hide."

Yes, he truly did.

"Well then, Sacred Beast, let's run a bit. I'm sure you must be exhausted, but..."

"Woof!"

"That's what I thought!"

And so, draped over Gyes' shoulder, I was carried off deep into the forest.

Ruijerd

RUIJERD WAS CLOSE to the city, but Rudeus still hadn't come back. Was he lost? No, he would've used magic to send a signal into the sky. Did that mean there was trouble instead? Ruijerd had disposed of every last human in that building, but perhaps Rudeus had run into backup that showed up from a different location. He should probably go back and check, just to be sure.

No. Rudeus wasn't a child. Even if an enemy did appear, he would be able to handle them. Rudeus' defenses could be weak, perhaps because he was young, but he wasn't so naive as to let his guard down in enemy territory.

Besides, right now he didn't have Eris to worry about. If Rudeus used the full extent of his powers, he couldn't be defeated. The only problem was that he was conflicted about taking a person's life. If he limited his powers too much, the tables might be turned on him. No...he wasn't that foolish, surely.

Rudeus didn't need his concern. Still, Ruijerd was troubled. If he continued into town with the children like this, he had a bad feeling about what might happen.

He'd faced similar circumstances many times before. He would rescue children from slave merchants and attempt to return them to the city, only to be mistaken as a kidnapper himself. His head was shaved and the jewel in his forehead was hidden, but he was poor with words. If the garrison stopped him for questioning, he had no confidence in his ability to explain what had happened.

Surely the humans of the city would take care of things if he just left the children there, right? No, Rudeus would definitely have some choice words for him if he did that.

"Mew, Mister, I'm sorry about before, mew."

While he worried, one of the girls came over and patted his leg. The other children looked similarly apologetic. It almost felt like they were the ones rescuing him.

"It's fine."

It really had been a long time since he'd used Beast God tongue, though. The last time he used it was... Hmm, just when was it again? He couldn't remember using it much at all since Laplace's War.

"The Sacred Beast is a symbol of our tribe, mew, so we just couldn't leave it behind, mew."

"So that's it. I didn't know that, but still, I apologize."
She smiled at Ruijerd when he said that. He really did
enjoy how children weren't so terrified of him. "Hmm..."

Suddenly his third eye sensed someone rapidly approaching. Their speed was incredible, and their aura
was strong. They came from the direction of the building
they'd left behind. Was it one of the smugglers' allies? But
they seemed too adept for that. *It couldn't be*, he thought.
Did they actually defeat Rudeus...?

"Get back." He had the children take cover behind
him as he readied his spear.

The victor would be the one who struck first. He
would bring them down in one blow.

Or so he thought, but Ruijerd's opponent stopped just
short of his reach. It was a male beastperson, holding a
thick hatchet in his hand. The man was clearly wary as
he took a stance of his own. He was elderly, but he had a
calm, composed and dignified air about him. The air of
a warrior. Yet Ruijerd would kill him if he were in league
with those bastards from before. Someone who let something like this happen to children of his own race was no
true warrior.

"Ah, Grandpa, mew!" The cat girl called out to the
older warrior and rushed to him.

"Tona! You're all right!"

The old warrior welcomed the girl into his arms, a look of relief crossing his face. Ruijerd lowered his spear. Apparently this man had come to save the children. Ruijerd was wrong to doubt him as a warrior; he was clearly an honorable man.

The dog-eared girl also seemed to know him, and dashed over to him.

"Tersena, you're safe too. I'm glad."

"That man over there saved us."

The old warrior put his sword away. Then he approached Ruijerd and bowed. It seemed he was still wary of Ruijerd, but that was to be expected.

"Thank you for saving my granddaughter."

"Sure."

"What's your name?"

"Ruijerd." *Superdia*, he thought to add, but he hesitated. If the man knew he was Superd, it would just put him on guard.

"Ruijerd, is it? I'm Gustav Dedoldia. I will repay this debt to you without fail. First, I must return these children to their parents."

"Yes, you should."

"But it's dangerous to make children walk at night. I'd like you to explain exactly what happened." As he said that, the elder started walking toward the town.

"Wait," Ruijerd called after him.

"What is it?"

"Did you look inside of the building?"

"I did. A depressing place that reeked of blood."

Ruijerd pressed on with his questions. "And no one was there?"

"There was one. A male in the form of a child. It seems he had a perverted grin as he fondled the Sacred Beast."

He realized who it was immediately. Rudeus. *So the kid still gets that grin on his face*, he thought. "That's my companion," Ruijerd said.

"Oh dear!"

"Don't tell me you killed him?"

It didn't matter if it was a misunderstanding that caused it. If they'd killed Rudeus, Ruijerd would have his revenge. He would see the children to their parents first, though. Eris too. That's right... Eris was alone right now. That worried him.

"I had him taken to our village so we could interrogate him about the location of his co-conspirators. But I will have him released immediately."

Rudeus, the idiot, had let his guard down. That boy... His defenses were always weak, even though his mental resilience was high. Then again, Ruijerd had no room to talk given that his mental resilience was third-class in comparison.

"Rudeus is a warrior. If you don't plan to kill him, there's no reason to hurry. Let's prioritize the children first."

The beastfolk did not torture as humans did. At most, they would strip him of his clothes and throw him in a cell. Rudeus had no qualms about people seeing him naked, after all. Just the other day, he'd said something strange to Ruijerd: "If Eris tries to peek in on me while I'm showering, you don't have to stop her."

Plus, there was Eris to worry about. Rudeus always entrusted Eris' protection to Ruijerd. He always worried more about her than about himself. Ruijerd was better off protecting her than chasing Rudeus down.

"I have my reasons for not exposing my true form," Ruijerd said. "I'd like you to lead the children on and find their parents."

"Hm... all right then." Gustav nodded, and Ruijerd headed back toward the city.

CHAPTER 7

Free Apartment

HELLO THERE. *My name's Rudeus and I used to be a shut-in.*

Currently I am checking out a new, free apartment that is the talk of the town. No security deposit, no key payment, no rent. A one-room space complete with two meals and spare time for a nap. The bed is made of bug-infested straw, which is a downside, but the price is cheap. After all, rent is free!

The toilet is a large jar set in the corner of the room. Once you've done your business and the jar is filled with excrement, you'll have to dump it in a hole on the opposite side of the room. There's no running water, so it is a little unhygienic, but you can get by with magic. If you are a magician like me, who can make warm water, your problems are completely solved!

There are only two meals. For modern-day folk, that might be too little. Still, this food is quite incredible, a lush land's regional specialty of fruits and vegetables. Meat as well. The seasoning is light, bringing out the natural flavor of the ingredients, which is enough to make anyone used to life on the Demon Continent smack their chops in delight.

Now for the apartment's primary feature: its security. Please, have a look at these durable iron bars. You can bang on them as much you like, pull at them as much you like, but they won't budge an inch. Their only weakness is that they can be pried open with magic.

There surely isn't a thief alive who would look at these bars and think, hey! I think I want to go in there! *Yet inside they will go, because this free apartment is a jail cell.*

Hung over Gyes' back, I continued my ride through the forest. Unable to move, I had no choice but to allow myself to be carried along. As we traveled through the shadows of the woods at breakneck speed, I saw something in the corner of my eye. There, between the blur of trees that flew by, was a blob of silver hair following us.

Still a pup, and yet the dog had quite the stamina. We'd been on the move for probably two or three hours by then. The beastfolk warrior known as Gyes had been running for quite a long time. He only stopped when we finally arrived wherever it was.

"Sacred Beast, please return to the house."

"Woof!" The ball of silver fur barked once before toddling off into the darkness.

I surveyed the surroundings by just using my eyes. The trees were closely clustered and I sensed no other person in the vicinity. However, I saw lights here and there above us in the trees. Gyes continued walking for a bit, approaching one of the trees.

With me still slung over his shoulder, he hooked his hands on a ladder I couldn't see and swiftly climbed. It seemed I was being taken into the treetops.

From there we entered a building. No one else was present. It was a deserted cabin made of wood. That's where Gyes stripped me of all my clothes.

What the hell was he doing to me? I couldn't even move my body!

He was lifted me up by the scruff of my neck and tossed me inside...something. A moment later, I heard the creak of iron and a *clang* as something fell. Then Gyes was gone, without any explanation. He didn't even interrogate me.

After a while, I could move my body again. I produced a small flame on the tip of my finger and used it to check my surroundings. I saw the durable bars and realized that this was a cell. I'd been thrown into a cell.

That was fine. Judging by the conversation they'd had, I knew this was going to happen. They'd mistaken me for a smuggler. That's why I didn't panic. This misunderstanding would soon be solved. Still, why the need to strip me? Come to think of it, those children had been stripped of all their clothes, too.

Maybe that was their custom here. Maybe beastfolk felt humiliated at being fully exposed. Although feeling embarrassed at being exposed wasn't a quality unique to their race. Stripping a captive to break them down mentally was a practice from time immemorial. This may have been a fantasy world, but even in my favorite book here, the female knight was relieved of her clothes when she was taken prisoner. It seemed all worlds had that in common.

"Now then..." Wrapped in darkness, I began to think.

For now, I would save speaking with them for tomorrow. Even if they didn't believe me, I would still be okay. The older man had apparently set off after Ruijerd, in which case he should have met up with the children by now. Ruijerd was an easy person to misunderstand, but the children would not forsake the warrior that had come to their aid, surely. The children would return safely, and I would no longer be mistaken for a smuggler.

The fact that I wasn't a smuggler, but had a complicated working relationship with them, was probably better left unsaid. Ruijerd never wanted to work with the smugglers either, so he wouldn't say anything that would get us in trouble. For now, the primary concern was my own safety. The older warrior said not to lay a hand on me until his return. That meant I was safe. They probably wouldn't set any tentacle monsters on me...right?

Either way, I felt like I finally understood the meaning behind Gallus' words. If this was what was going to happen to them, they surely would have been in a lot of trouble.

An entire day passed as I was busy thinking those things. Time was fleeting. The morning of the day after I was thrown into this cell, a guard appeared. It was a woman. She had the build of a warrior, and yet she was more slender than Ghislaine. Although her chest was just as huge.

I told her, "I've been falsely charged, I didn't do anything." I went on to explain that I wasn't associated with that smuggling organization, that I just happened to find out those children were being held in that building and that, fueled by righteous indignation, I set about freeing them.

The woman did not hear a word I said. Instead she carried a bucket of water to my cell and dumped it over my head as I protested. It was freezing cold, and now I looked like a drowned rat. The woman then glared at me as if I were nothing more than garbage.

"Pervert...!"

A shiver ran through me. There I was, naked, with this beautiful animal-eared older woman ravaging me with her eyes. Not only had she poured freezing water over me, but she'd also verbally abused me. This was what it meant to break someone down psychologically.

It seemed they had no intention of following the older warrior's command. Just what would happen to me now...? Ahh, God (Roxy), give unto me your protection! And no, Man-God, I don't mean you!

"Achoo!"

All joking aside, I really did want some clothes. For now, I would use the fire spell Burn In Place to keep myself warm so I didn't catch a cold.

Day two.

Ruijerd still hadn't come to rescue me. After being left naked for two whole days, my anxiety was beginning to rear its ugly head. I wondered if something happened to Ruijerd. Did he end up fighting that older warrior?

Or did things with Gallus go sour? Or perhaps something had happened to Eris and he was seeing to that?

I was anxious. Incredibly anxious. That was why I was constructing an escape plan. Early in the afternoon, once I was done eating, I started to quietly use my magic. I mixed fire and wind, creating a warm air current that buffeted the room and made the entire area nice and toasty. The amply endowed guard grew sleepy and began to drift off. How easy.

I unlocked the cell door and checked to see that no one else was around as I slipped out of the building.

"Ooh..."

The sight that spread out before me was like something straight out of a dream. There was a settlement built above the trees. The buildings were all set among the treetops, scaffolding around each tree to give space for walking. There were also bridges that connected the trees together so you could come and go without having to climb up and down ladders.

There was really nothing on the ground below. I could see what looked to be a simple shack and the traces of a field, but they didn't seem to be in use. Apparently no one lived there.

There weren't that many people. I could see a few beastfolk here and there, bustling about on the scaffolding. If a person walked across a bridge, then they would be fully exposed to anyone below, and anyone who moved below would be fully exposed to those above.

Right now I was, in every sense of the word, fully exposed. It would be difficult to escape without being seen. Although if I were caught, I could still run away. If I didn't think about the consequences, I could just set fire to a nearby tree and escape into the forest in the ensuing chaos.

Ah, the forest. I didn't know my way out there. Gyes had run at top speed for a long time, so we had to be quite a distance from the town. Even if I ran with all my might, heading straight as the crow flies, it would probably take me about six hours. And I was sure I would get lost on the way.

I could use earth magic to build a tower, giving me a high vantage point to look out from. That was an option. Of course, if I did something that attention-catching, Gyes would be on my tail immediately.

I still didn't know what was behind that magic he used. If I couldn't come up with a way to counter it in a fight, I might lose. Plus, next time he might cut my legs off so I wouldn't be able to run. Perhaps it was better that I wait a little longer for my circumstances to change.

It had just been a couple of days. That older warrior hadn't returned yet. Ruijerd might still be searching for those children's parents. There was no need to be impatient, I decided, and headed back into my cell.

Day three.

The food that guard brought was delicious. It was as expected—the land here was so rich with nature. It was a remarkable difference from the Demon Continent. The meals consisted of either a wild grass soup or scraps of grilled meat that were tough to tear into, but both were delicious. Perhaps it was because I had grown used to the Demon Continent's food. If this was the grub they offered someone in a cell, then no doubt the rest of the settlement was having a feast.

When I complimented the food, the guard flicked her tail and brought me seconds. Based on her reaction, she was probably the one who made it. Although she still wouldn't say a word to me as usual.

Day four.

I was bored. There was nothing to do. Maybe I could create something with my magic, but if I did they might gag me or bind my wrists. Then there really would be nothing I could do. There was no reason to risk robbing myself of what little freedom I had.

Day five.

I got a roommate today. He was carried in by two beastfolk on either side. They promptly tossed him inside, sending him tumbling with a swift kick to the rear.

"Dammit! You should treat me better than that!"

The beastfolk ignored his cries and left.

The man gingerly rubbed at his behind, hissing in pain as he slowly turned his around. I greeted him in a reclining Buddha pose, stretched out on my side with my head propped up against my hand. "Welcome to life's final destination." Of course, I was completely naked.

The man stared at me, gobsmacked. He looked like an adventurer. His clothes were all black, with leather protectors fastened at the joints. He was unarmed, of course. He had long sideburns and a monkey face like Lupin the Third. Calling it a monkey's face wasn't a metaphor, though. He was a demon.

"What's wrong, newbie? See something amiss?" I asked.

"N-no, not exactly how I'd describe it." He looked at me in confusion.

Come on, I'll get embarrassed if you stare like that, I thought.

"You're naked, but you act awfully full of yourself."

"Hey, newbie, better watch your mouth. I've been here longer than you. That means I'm the master of this cell, your elder. Show some respect," I commanded.

"Y-yeah."

"Your answer should be 'yes, sir'!"

"Yes, sir."

Why, you ask, was I acting so full of myself in front of someone I had just met for the first time? Because I was bored, of course.

"Unfortunately there's no mat for you to sit on, so just sit over here somewhere."

"Y-yes, sir."

"Now then, newbie. Why were you thrown in here?" I tried to sound tough as I asked.

I expected that my impertinence despite being younger might infuriate him, but he just answered back with a dumbfounded look on his face, "They caught me trying to swindle them."

"Oho, gambling, is it? Restricted Rock-Paper-Scissors? Steel Frame Crossing?"

"What the hell is that? No, dice."

"Dice, huh?" He probably used rigged dice that would only land on four, five or six. "A boring crime to be taken in for."

"What about you?" he asked.

"You can tell just by looking, can't you? Public indecency."

"What the hell is that?"

"While naked, I put my arms around a silver-colored pup, and then they threw me in here," I explained.

"Ah! I heard the rumors. Some sex fiend assaulted the Doldia's Sacred Beast!"

Someone out there was sure being cheeky with their words. To begin with, that was a false accusation. Not that I would gain anything by claiming as much here.

"Newbie, if you're a man then you understand, right? The lust one feels for an adorable creature."

"No clue." His eyes changed, and now he looked at me with suspicion. Well, they hadn't really changed. His eyes had been like that from the start.

"So, newbie, what's your name?"

"Geese," he answered.

"You a military man? Eaten more meals as a soldier than there are stars in the sky?"

"Military man? No, I'm just an adventurer, I guess. Been one for a while."

Geese. Let's see, I felt like I'd heard that name before. But where? I couldn't remember. It seemed like there were a lot of people with that name, so he probably wasn't the Geese I knew.

"I'm Rudeus. I'm younger than you, but here, I'm your boss."

"Yeah, yeah." Geese shrugged his shoulders, flopped over where he stood and propped his head up. "Hm? Rudeus… I've heard that name before."

"I'm sure lots of people have that name."

"Eh, probably right."

Now we were both doing the reclining Buddha pose as we faced each other, although one of us was naked. Wasn't that a bit strange, though? Why was I, the greatest person occupying this cell, naked while the newbie still had his clothes on? Strange. Very strange indeed.

"Hey, newbie."

"What is it, boss?" he asked.

"That vest of yours looks warm. Hand it over."

"Wha…?" Geese looked displeased as he said, "Fine, here," and peeled the vest off before tossing it at me. Maybe he was actually good at looking out for people, contrary to my initial impression.

"Ah, thank you so very much," I said, sounding ever so polite.

"So you *can* show gratitude," he observed.

"Of course. I've been rocking it freestyle for days now. For the first time in a while I feel like a person again."

"Boss, you don't have to talk so fancy."

Thus I achieved the appearance of a snot-nosed brat straight out of the Edo period.

Our guard watched us with a sullen look on her face, but she didn't say anything.

"Now I can feel your warmth radiating from this vest."

"Hey, don't tell me you're into men, too?" Geese asked.

"Of course not," I replied. "With women I'll go as high as forty-year-olds, but unless you look like a woman, I've got no interest in men."

"So you're fine with it if they look like a woman..." Geese stared at me with disbelief. But if he met a woman who was his type, one who extracted his Excalibur like Arthur, then he'd become a Merlin too. In the sexual sense, of course.

"By the way, newbie, there's something I want to ask you."

"What is it?"

"Where is this place?" I asked.

"A cell in the Doldia's village in the Great Forest."

"And who am I?"

"Rudeus. The naked pervert who put his hands on a pup," he answered.

Aha! But I wasn't naked anymore! Also, that was a false charge. I wasn't a pervert.

"And what is a demon like you doing in the Doldia's village, gambling your life away?"

Geese explained. "Ahh, well, one of my acquaintances from a long time ago was a Doldia, so I came on the off chance I might meet her."

"Did you?"

"I did not," he said.

"So even though they weren't here, you gambled? Swindled?" I pressed on.

"Didn't think I'd get caught."

This guy was hopeless. But maybe he wasn't useless.

"Newbie. What else can you do besides swindle?"

"I can do anything," he said.

"Oho, like you can make a dragon with your bare hand and knock someone down with it?"

"No, that's impossible," he replied. "I suck at fighting."

"Could you take on like one hundred women at once then?" I asked.

"One is plenty, two at the most."

For my last question, I lowered my voice enough so that the guard wouldn't be able to hear us and said, "Could you make it to the city if you got out of here?"

He lifted himself upright, glanced quickly at the guard, and then scratched his head. He brought his face closer to mine and spoke in a hushed whisper. "Are you trying to run away?"

"My companion isn't coming, so yes."

"Ahh, yeah, that's... Well, that sucks."

Hey you, knock it off, I thought. *If you put it like that, you make it sound like my friends have abandoned me.*

Ruijerd would never leave me behind like that. I was sure that he was looking everywhere for those kids' parents right now. That, or something had occurred and he was in trouble. Maybe he was waiting for my help.

"Run off on your own then. It's got nothin' to do with me," Geese said.

I explained, "I don't know the way to the nearest town from here."

"Then how did you get here?"

"I saved some kids who were kidnapped by smugglers," I told him.

"Saved them?"

"And while we were there I took off this collar that had been put on that pup, and when I did this beastperson suddenly appeared and shouted at me. Then I couldn't move anymore and they brought me here."

Bewildered, Geese scratched at his head again. Perhaps I hadn't explained it well enough. "Ahh, so that's what happened. You were falsely accused?"

"Exactly."

"I see. Yeah, then of course you'd wanna run."

"So that's why I'd like you to lend me a hand," I said.

"Don't wanna," he replied. "Run off by yourself if you want to so bad."

He could say that all he liked, but it still didn't help me find the way. It would be no laughing matter if I got myself lost in the woods on my way to go help Ruijerd.

"But if it's really a false charge you should be fine. They'll understand."

"I hope you're right," I said.

From my point of view, Gyes wasn't the kind who listened to people. Although it was the truth that I had helped those kids escape. If they came back, then the false charge against me would be dropped.

"Then I guess I better wait a little longer."

"Yeah, you should," he agreed. "Running away doesn't solve anything." Geese flopped back onto his side.

I decided to wait like he suggested. Fortunately, I still had options left. If it came to it, I could engulf this whole area in a sea of flames and escape. I felt bad for the Doldia tribe, but they were the ones who had arrested me on false charges after all, so we were even.

Even so, Ruijerd sure was taking his sweet time. I assumed it was just taking that long for him to find the children's parents, but still, this was too much.

Day six.

This apartment was truly comfortable to live in. Food was provided for us. It was equipped with good air conditioning (albeit man-made), and while at first I thought it was boring because there was nothing to do, now I had a conversation partner.

The bed had been infested with bugs, but thanks to the warm air I created with my magic, they'd all been eradicated. The toilet was in its usual sad state, but it was kind of titillating to think of that pretty, older animal-eared woman cleaning up after me.

Still, I felt anxious about the fact that I was getting no news. It had been nearly a week since I was brought here. Wasn't Ruijerd really overdue? Wasn't it normal to assume that something must have happened? Some kind of trouble that Ruijerd couldn't handle on his own?

I had no idea what help I would be if I went. Perhaps it would already be too late. Even so, I needed to go. Tomorrow. No, the day after tomorrow. I would wait until the day after tomorrow.

Once that day came, I would reduce this village to a flaming field. Or not, because I would feel bad about doing that. Instead, I would take the guard as my captive and run.

Day seven.

This was my last day living in this cell. In the depths of my mind I was carefully crafting a plan, while outwardly I just sluggishly ate and slept. I couldn't keep this up—the shut-in mentality from my previous life would make its reappearance. Tomorrow, I would need to psyche myself up.

"Yo, newbie..." I called out to Geese in my usual thug style as I settled down on the ground.

"What?"

"Is this the only cell in the village?"

"Why are you asking that?" he replied.

"Well, it's just that they don't normally throw two people in the same cell for no reason, right?" I reasoned.

"They don't normally use this cell. Criminals are usually shipped off to Zant Port."

Shipped off to Zant Port, huh? So the Doldia Tribe only threw special criminals into this cell, then? I was mistaken for a smuggler and also falsely accused of attempted bestiality on their Sacred Beast. It must have been really important to the village to have such a special title. That made me an even more extraordinary criminal.

But wait.

"Then why were you put in here? You were arrested for swindling, right?"

"Don't ask me. Probably because it happened in the village and it was no big deal, right?"

"So that's the reason why?"

"That's the reason why," he answered.

Something felt a little off to me. I scratched at my side, then scratched at my stomach. While I was at it, I scratched at my back. For some reason, I was itchy. As soon as I realized that, I looked down and saw something hopping. A single flea, leaping.

"Gaaah! This vest, it's got bugs coming out of it!"

"Hm? Oh yeah, I haven't washed it in a while," Geese said.

"Then wash it!" I peeled it off and flung it away. It flapped as it flew, sending bugs scattering onto the floor. I immediately exterminated them all with the heat of my air magic. Darn pests...!

"Hey, I've been watching you do that for a bit now. Sure is amazing. Just how *do* you do it, though?"

"Voiceless casting, using magic without an incantation," I explained.

"...Huh. Without an incantation. That really is incredible."

Yeah, and now that I was thinking about how those insects had been swarming inside that vest, my entire body suddenly felt extremely itchy. I would have to heal each bite one by one. Perhaps it was because I wore nothing under the vest, but my back seemed to have a ridiculous amount of bites. That's right, my back. Right where my hand couldn't reach. Gaah!

"Yo, newbie."

"What?"

"Come over here and scratch my back," I commanded. "It itches like hell."

"Yeah, yeah."

I sat with my legs crossed and Geese came up from behind me. He began scratching away.

"Yeah, there, right there. Oh yeah, you're really good at this."

"I told you, right?" he said. "I can do anything. If you want, I can massage your shoulders for you, too." As Geese said that, he moved his hands to my shoulders. Dang. He really was good at this.

I instinctively straightened my back. "Ooh, you're really good. That feels great. Ahh, next time go a little lower. Mm, yeah, right there...hm?"

Just then I realized something was very off. But what? Something was different from the usual. "Hey, newbie..."

"What now? Want me to go lower? You want me to scratch your ass, too?"

"No, don't you feel like something's weird?"

"Yeah, boss, you're weird in the head," he answered.

"Aside from that!" I snapped. How rude.

"Well, yeah...that guard lady hasn't come in."

Yes, exactly. Normally this would be time for our noon meal. A time when we would eat our delicious, delicious food before putting our hands together in thanks. But we had no clock, so it was possible that I was just getting the time wrong. But my aching belly seemed to think it was lunchtime.

"Also, it sounds like it's pretty noisy outside."

"Really?" I listened carefully and sure enough, I heard fighting in the distance. But it also felt like it could just be my imagination.

"Also it's a little hot."

"Now that you mention it, it's true, today is awfully hot," I realized.

"Also, isn't it a bit smoky in here?"

"Now that you mention it..."

He was right. A thin veil of gray smoke had filtered in. The smoke was spilling in from the skylight and the front entrance.

"Newbie, lend me your shoulder."

"Guess I got no choice. Here you go."

Geese lifted me up onto his shoulders, and from the slightly higher vantage of the skylight window, I peered outside.

The forest was burning.

CHAPTER 8

Fire Emergency

"IT'S A FIRE!" I screamed and leaped down from Geese's shoulders.

"Mmm? Wait just a—hey!" Geese leapt to the skylight and peeked out. "You weren't jokin' around! Wh-what should we do, boss?!"

What was going on? Here I had been planning to leave the following day, and now if I didn't take action, we'd be baked like a couple of cakes.

"We're getting out of here, of course! And we'll use the chaos to escape!" I declared.

"But how are we going to get out?! The door is locked, you know!"

"Don't worry," I said. "That's not a problem!" I slipped toward the door and fished out the key I had hidden to unlock it.

"Whoa! When did you have time to steal a key?"

"Just something I prepared in case something like this happened, back when I first started planning my escape!"

Geese said, "I see, so you're the type of criminal who waits until everyone's distracted by a crisis before you strike."

How rude. It wasn't like I'd stolen anything. I just made a copy of the original, that's all. In any case, I shoved the key into the lock and turned it until it clicked as the door opened. Now for the prison break challenge! "Okay, let's go!"

"Yeah!" Geese chimed.

The door opened and a wave of hot air slapped us in the face. Flames danced violently as the blaze, bright and fierce, devoured the forest with a voracious hunger. The houses on the treetops were engulfed, threatening to crumble.

"This is really bad," Geese muttered.

No kidding. I nodded in agreement.

People were probably banned from lighting fires in this forest, but no doubt some wise guy decided to sit in bed and have a smoke, thereby causing all of this. I didn't know who he was, but we would be able to escape thanks to him, so I wasn't going to complain.

"Okay, newbie, which way is Zant Port?"

"What? How the hell would I know?" he shouted at me as he looked around.

"What do you mean you don't know?" I shouted back. "You said you knew the way, didn't you?"

"Not when we're surrounded by fire on all sides!"

Hmm...well, now that he mentioned it, he was right. After all, the phrase "smoke screen" would have no meaning if you could just see straight through black smoke and crimson flames.

So what to do? Put out the flames? No, we needed the confusion of the flames to escape. If we put them out we'd be found immediately. On top of that, we might be mistaken for arsonists. How about temporarily fleeing outside the range of the fire so we could look for a way back to the town? Wait...could we even escape without putting out the fire?

"What are we gonna do?! We're running out of escape routes!"

Just how big was the fire in the first place? Even if we ran and ran, there was a possibility we might not be able to escape the enveloped area.

"Hey, boss! Look!" Geese pointed.

He was pointing at a child. A small, cat-eared child. They were rubbing their eyes and coughing as they tottered in our direction, having inhaled some of the smoke.

Nearby, a tree's foliage burst into flames that crackled as the whole thing threatened to collapse. The child looked at the tree, but it was all happening so suddenly that they could only look on, dumbfounded.

"Watch out!" I cried out, instantly unleashing wind magic to fling the tree out of the way.

The smoke had blurred their eyesight, but the child saw us and approached. "H-help...me..."

I took them into my arms and used water magic to clean their eyes. They also had some light burns on their body, so I used healing magic as well. I wasn't sure what I should be doing, but I hoped that would help for now at least. What were they doing here anyway? Had they simply failed to escape?

"Don't tell me the villagers haven't completely evacuated yet?"

"Definitely possible," Geese said. "Fires are pretty rare as the rain season approaches...whoa!"

Another tree collapsed. A small house that had been above us was also collapsing, scattering bits of flame like powder. It looked like no effort was being made to put out the fire. If I kept lingering, I would be in danger, too. Still, I couldn't just leave this child behind and run.

"All right..." I made my decision. "Newbie, do you know where the center of the village is?"

"Yeah, I know where that is...but what are you gonna do?"

"I'm going to do them a favor so they'll feel indebted to me!"

After I said that, Geese grinned, gathered the child in his arms, and broke into a run. "Okay then, this is the way. Follow me!"

I moved to follow...but then remembered my clothes. They might still be hidden in that little jail. I quickly used my water magic to engulf the building in ice before I followed Geese.

The flames had yet to reach the heart of the village. Still, I hadn't expected what I saw. Beastfolk were trying to flee. They were panicked, shrieking and screaming as they ran to and fro. That part I had expected, but for some reason there were also humans in battle gear chasing the beastfolk down. Farther off I could see what looked like the beastfolk warriors fighting with humans. Even farther off, I saw robust-looking men carrying a child under either arm, probably trying to cart them somewhere.

What was this? What the heck was going on?

Geese spoke. "Hmm, I thought something fishy was going on..."

"Newbie, do you know what's going on?" I asked.

"Just what it looks like. Those guys are attacking the beastfolk."

True. That was exactly what it looked like.

"I'd guess they're the ones who set the fires, too," Geese added.

So they attacked by setting fires. Almost like bandits. There really were some cruel people out there. On the other hand, the beastfolk had imprisoned me for a week when I was innocent of any crime. People did say curses were like chickens: They came home to roost.

"Still, this is...a bit much."

Girls were being dragged off by men. A child was screaming, calling out for their mother, who tried to give chase only to be cut down. The beastfolk warriors tried to prevent the kidnappings, but their movements were dulled. Smoke had hampered their vision and sense of smell. The humans overwhelmed them in numbers, and the beastfolk found themselves surrounded, forced into a bitter fight.

Terrible, truly terrible.

"So...boss."

"What is it?"

"Which side are you gonna help?"

I glanced at the scene again. Another beastfolk warrior fell. Human men forced their way into the building that warrior had been protecting and emerged dragging a child by their hair.

It was obvious which was the side of justice. But which one was evil to me?

I had no idea who these humans were. Given that they were kidnapping children, they were most likely working with slave traders or smugglers, to whom I did owe a debt. They brought Ruijerd across the sea for me. Although we'd offset it by murdering everyone in that base, so I considered us even.

In comparison, the beastfolk had imprisoned me on a false charge. They wouldn't listen to anything I said. They stripped me and threw freezing cold water on me, then just left me in my cell. On an emotional level, I had a poor impression of them.

Still. Even still, this scene before me...was nauseating.

"The beastfolk, of course," I said finally.

"Haha! Now you're talkin'!" Geese said before lifting a sword off the nearest dead body and taking a stance. "All right, leave the front line to me! I may not be much with a sword, but I can at least be a wall for you!"

"Yeah, I'm counting on you to protect me," I said and lifted both hands to the sky.

First, I had to put out these flames. I used Squall, an advanced water magic spell. I channeled mana into my right hand, conjuring gray clouds in the sky. I made sure the scope and power of the spell was large. I had no idea how far the fire had spread, but I could probably put out most of it if I expanded my spell as much as possible. I also increased the precipitation rate so it would come down like a vast downpour.

I manipulated the clouds just as I'd learned to do when casting Cumulonimbus. I compressed my mana until it formed a cloud, then I swelled that cloud bigger and bigger without letting a single drop of rain fall. No one noticed me standing there, my arms raised toward the sky. And thanks to the black smoke, they didn't notice the clouds growing above, either.

"Okay!" Once the clouds were big enough, I released the hold my mana had on them.

"Whoa..." Geese reflexively looked up as the rain began to come down at us like a waterfall.

It was a deluge that beat down upon everyone. In seconds the area was flooded. Flames hissed in the distance as they dissipated. People looked at the sky, some suspicious about the sudden rainfall. Soon they noticed me standing with both hands raised. The nearest human whipped out his sword and started running my way.

"H-hey, what are you gonna do, boss, they're coming!"

"Quagmire!" As I spoke the spell's name, a muddy

pit opened below them. Unable to wade through it, the men lost their balance and collapsed. "Stone Cannon!" I cast the next spell without a moment's delay, hammering them with my earth spell and knocking them out. A piece of cake. These guys were nothing special.

"Ooh...that was amazing, boss!"

I ignored Geese's praise and moved forward. The humans were here, there, and everywhere. I started on one side and began pummeling them with my stone cannon. I would continue this gradual onslaught and then take back the kids who had been abducted. If Ruijerd and Eris were here to chase after the thugs, the work would have gone a lot faster, but I had to be cautious since I was going it alone.

Well, not quite. I did have Geese with me. Although he seemed rather useless skills-wise, so I didn't expect he'd be of much help.

"Hey, there's a magician here! He put out the fire!"

"Dammit! What the hell?!"

"Kill him! Use your numbers and don't let him cast!"

As I got distracted, human warriors came charging at me, one after the other.

"Stone Cannon!" I turned my hand toward them and pummeled them with my spell. One, two, three... Oh crap, not only did they have leadership now, but their numbers were overwhelming.

"D-dammit! Bring it on, then! I won't let you put a hand on my boss!" Geese cried out valiantly, although he was gradually retreating to the side. Useless.

What about me? Should I fall back too? I wondered.

At that very moment, a brown shadow flew in front of me. "I don't know who you are, but thank you for the help!"

He spoke in Beast-God tongue. He was a beastman with a bushy dog's tail who already had his sword drawn, and he cut down one of the men coming toward us. His single stroke sliced cleanly through and sent the human's head flying.

"We won't be defeated by your ilk, now that the rain has cleaned my face and my nose is working properly!"

Ooh, how heroically spoken! But it was just as he said: All the beastfolk in the area were making a comeback.

"Little magician! Please help us gather our warriors and take back our children!"

"Got it!"

The beastman in front of me seemed a little surprised that I'd answered in the Beast God tongue, but he nodded vigorously and howled into the distance. Several more beastfolk leapt from the trees or the thicket to join us. Others who had defeated their foes raced over to us on all fours.

"Gunther, Gilbad, come with me. We're going to work with this magician to rescue the children. The rest of you, protect this area."

"Woo!" They all nodded and dispersed. I also moved, losing sight of the warrior who had first appeared before me. Geese followed along behind me.

The warriors largely ran straight ahead uninterrupted, occasionally lifting their noses to sniff the air. If we met a human along the way, they quickly dispatched them.

That was when we heard a shrill cry that sounded like a dog.

On inspection, we found a beastperson being driven into a corner by three humans. The humans seemed to enjoy their unfair numerical advantage, like cats tormenting a mouse. That also meant their guard was down.

I immediately knocked one unconscious with a stone cannon. The warrior who had been running beside me leaped forward and attacked one of the others. The last human, panicked by the fact that his comrades had been killed so suddenly, was cut down by the very beastperson they had been torturing.

"Laklana! You all right?!"

"Y-yes, Warrior Gimbal! You saved me!" The beastperson who had been cornered was a woman. A female warrior. She was covered in wounds thanks to her fight.

I was about to cast a healing spell over her when I suddenly realized I recognized her.

She was similarly startled when she got a look at me. "Gimbal! This boy is—"

"Not our enemy. He conjured the rain just a moment ago. He's dressed a little funny, but he's helping us."

"What?" she gasped.

Her confusion wasn't just because only a fur vest covered my naked (or rather half-naked) body. I knew her. I only just found out her name, but I knew those ample breasts and skilled cooking hands. She was the one who had guarded our cell.

She looked between Gimbal and me, her face turning pale. She probably remembered her poor treatment of me and realized the mistake she'd made.

Don't worry. I don't really hold it against you, I thought. *People sometimes misunderstand and make mistakes. I am Rudeus, the enlightened and compassionate!*

That aside, she needed to let me cast a bit of healing on her.

She looked conflicted as I healed her, wondering what she should do, if she should apologize or not.

Before I could finish healing her, Gimbal yelled, "Laklana, you are to return and guard the Sacred Beast!"

"A-all right...!" She gave no thanks. Although it did

seem she had something she wanted to say, even as she followed Gimbal's orders and ran off.

Our pursuit continued. We left the village and entered the forest. At this point, one of the warriors let me ride on their back because I was too slow. From that position, I became a stone cannon launching machine.

Shoulder Equipment: Rudeus.

A piece of equipment that, upon encountering an enemy, will deflect any attack through use of the Eye of Foresight, and also automatically knock down enemies.

Granted, I only put in enough power to knock those men unconscious, but the beastfolk could deliver the necessary finishing blow for me.

"That's the last one!"

The last human halted the moment we caught up, dropping his cargo so he could draw his sword. The cargo was a young boy with a bag over his head and his hands bound behind him. Judging from how limply he fell to the ground, he was likely already unconscious. The man knelt beside him and put a sword to the child's neck. A hostage, huh?

"Grrrr...!" Gimbal and the others snarled and surrounded the warrior, maintaining their distance.

The man seemed unperturbed as he scanned the scene, until his eyes finally landed on me. "Kennel Master, what the hell are you doing here?"

I recognized his bearded face. Gallus. The man who smuggled Ruijerd across the sea for me, the one who entrusted us with a job. The one who worked for that smuggling organization.

"Well, a lot happened...and you, Mister Gallus, why are you here?"

"Why? Hmph, this was my plan from the very beginning."

Gimbal and the others looked between us, wondering if we were acquaintances or comrades.

Ugh...I didn't really want to talk about this here, but I couldn't keep silent, either. "What do you mean by that?"

Gallus hocked and spat. "There's no need for me to tell you."

Well, that was true. But this was a little odd. "You're the one who asked us to save the beastfolk children. You said it'd cause trouble for you in the future otherwise. But here you are kidnapping them...so what exactly are your intentions?"

Gallus smirked and looked around. Even though he had three beastfolk warriors, myself, and Geese surrounding him, he still seemed relaxed. "Yeah, the brats were one thing, but if they kidnapped the Doldia's Sacred Beast too, that would really get us into trouble."

Apparently that pup was the problem. I wish he'd said

so from the beginning. He could've at least told me to release the dog.

"I thought we had a good plan going. We timed it right and leaked information to the Doldia's band of warriors so you'd run into each other. Then while the Superd massacred them all, we would sneak in, attack their settlement and steal the rest of their children."

"..."

"It'd be too late by the time their warriors realized there was an attack on the village. Once the rainy season hit, they'd be unable to make a move and would just have to cry themselves to sleep at night since they couldn't come after us."

During the rainy season, most people couldn't leave the village. The smugglers must have thought they could cut off their pursuers by timing it just right.

"You sure do go about things in a very indirect manner," I said.

"I told you, we aren't a united organization. Can't let my comrades get ahead of me."

How vulgar. He would release his comrades' slaves, then sell his own. He would see a huge profit while they wouldn't get even a penny. His rank would rise while his failed comrades' would sink. After carefully sowing his seeds, Gallus would reap the rewards.

"Did you know, Kennel Master? These Doldia brats sell at an exceptionally high price. Some perverted noble family in the Asura Kingdom adores them and those guys will pay a lot of coin for them."

Ah, yes. I think I know which family he was talking about.

"It didn't go exactly to plan, but your Superd kept the Doldia warrior band tied up at Zant Port. Why is it, then, that you're here?"

"I screwed things up and got caught."

"Oh yeah, then why don't you join me?"

At those words, Gimbal turned his gaze toward me. He seemed to understand the tongue of men to some degree, and he watched me warily. I really wished he wouldn't do that.

"Mister Gallus... Sorry, but when I rescue children, I'm not Kennel Master Ruijerd. I'm Ruijerd of the Superd tribe. And Ruijerd never forgives those who would sell children as slaves."

"Hah, so Dead End likes to pretend it's on the side of justice, huh?"

"That's what I'd like people to believe."

Negotiations had failed.

Gallus kept his sword trained on the child's neck as he stood. He cast a look around at Gimbal and his men, who were trying to surround Gallus, and chuckled. "I see... Well, Kennel Master, you've made a mistake."

I literally just told you I'm not the Kennel Master, I'm Ruijerd, I quipped in my head.

Two of Gimbal's men slipped behind Gallus, sneaky as cats, creeping up on him.

"Five of you aren't enough to defeat me."

The three of them jumped on him almost instantaneously. From behind and to the right came Warrior A, slashing; and to the left, Warrior B swept in, attempting to rescue the child. Gimbal used that beat to attack Gallus from the front.

Against these agile beasts, Gallus moved almost sluggishly. First he launched the child at Gimbal. Gimbal caught the kid in his arms while Warrior B, who had now lost his target, fumbled for a split second. It was in that moment, using the momentum he'd gained from discarding the child, that Gallus pivoted around and butchered Warrior A. His blade was a common longsword, which he used to deflect the oncoming attack before burying it into Warrior A's chest.

He pulled his sword free while backing into Warrior B just as the latter fumbled his attack. At this point, Warrior B and Gimbal were both in a direct line in front of Gallus, and Gimbal's arms were preoccupied with the child he'd recovered, so he couldn't move. From out of nowhere, Gallus drew a short sword with his left hand and drove it deep into Warrior B's chest. Then he used the warrior's body as a shield and charged right at Gimbal.

Gimbal slipped the child under the crook of his arm and tried to intercept Gallus, but it was already too late. Gallus unleashed his attack between the gap of his shield's legs, piercing Gimbal. As Gimbal dropped the child and began to collapse, Gallus instantly sliced his blade clean through his opponent's neck.

Swift, precise and over in seconds. I didn't even have a chance to help. While I stared dumbfounded, the beast-folk warriors spilled blood from their mouths before collapsing where they stood.

Are you serious? I thought in disbelief.

"H-hey, boss, this is bad. That's North God Style right there. And also Atofe-style. No clever tricks, just a raw fighting style that comes from being experienced in facing multiple opponents in battle."

Gallus reacted to the panic in Geese's voice with a laugh. "You know your stuff, monkey man. That's right, I'm the Cleaner, the North Saint Gallus." By the time Gallus said that, he already had his hostage back in his grasp.

This was bad. I didn't think he was as strong as Ruijerd, but at that rank, he was probably still more than I could handle. Just how much could I fight him with my Eye of Foresight?

"Pretty interesting, isn't it? The North God Style even has a tactic for fighting while using a hostage."

I remembered how my father in this world, Paul, used to disparage the North God Style at length. Now it made sense. I could understand why someone would hate a style that had battle tactics like this. It was a disgrace. Truly underhanded. I wanted him to fight fair.

"Well, bring it on, Kennel Master. Or are you a coward who's lost the stomach for it, so now you'll let me go?"

No amount of mentally criticizing him would change our circumstances. Perhaps I should just let him go? I wasn't like Ruijerd. I didn't have such a strong sense of justice that I would put my life on the line to save children I didn't even know. The only thing worth risking my life for was Eris.

"What, so you really aren't going to come at me? Okay then, that's fine. Does us both a favor."

In contrast, Gallus seemed to be wary of me. Maybe he'd witnessed me using magic to stop the forest fires. I had also shown him I could use magic without chanting. He might come lunging at me the moment he saw any indication that I was going to cast something.

No matter how great Gallus' estimation of my abilities

was, there was nothing I could do right now. Even if I used my Eye of Foresight, defeating a master swordsman like Gallus without harming the hostage was most likely impossible. If attacking him meant the loss of my own precious life, then I had no choice but to let him walk.

"All right," Gallus started to say. "See ya around then, Kennel Master. If we meet again somewhere—"

"RAAAAH!"

At that moment, just as he let down his guard and hauled his hostage up into his arms, a white blur tackled Gallus from the side. It bit into his sword-wielding hand.

"Gaaaah! What's this?!"

A dog. That enormous white Shiba Inu had suddenly leaped from the bushes and sunk its fangs into Gallus.

I moved reflexively, using magic to create a shockwave between Gallus and the hostage.

"Guh?!"

This created a recoil that forced the two of them apart. The Sacred Beast also distanced itself at the moment of impact.

Gallus retrieved his sword and turned toward me. "Dammit, Kennel Master! I knew you'd come at me!" His eyes burned with hatred, as if I were the one who had launched the initial attack. "It's just like the rumors said!

You really do set your dogs loose on people. What an underhanded trick!"

What kind of rumor was that?! No, leaving that aside, the more important thing was that I was actually trying to help Gallus there.

"Grrrr...!" The Sacred Beast was ready for battle. Before I'd even noticed, it had come to my side, taking up a supportive stance with its body crouched low.

"Heh heh, just what I'd expect from you, boss. Take care of my ashes for me after I die." The newbie, Geese, positioned himself just slightly in front of me, timidly holding his sword at the ready.

Gallus didn't let his guard drop for an instant as he took a stance directly facing me. It seemed like I couldn't back down now even if I wanted to. Oh well. I did decide I would make the beastfolk feel indebted to me, so why not see it through to the bitter end?

"Sorry, Gallus. But Dead End's Ruijerd can't be the bad guy."

The words sounded heroic enough, but my situation wasn't ideal. We were currently three against one, but so were the beastfolk warriors, who had certainly looked stronger than our current group, and they were all slaughtered instantly. Right now Gallus didn't have his hostage, but all we had was an unreliable group of three:

the newbie, the pup and me. I dearly wished Ruijerd was among our number, but... No, this was a good opportunity for me to practice.

"Boss...buy me a little bit of time."

Just as I was mentally preparing myself, the newbie whispered to me. Did he have some kind of plan?

"Since he's a North God Style swordsman, I think I have something that will trip him up."

"...Okay." I stepped out directly in front of him. So this meant I was going to face off directly with a Saint-tier swordsman? Crap, my heart was pounding furiously. *Calm down, just calm down*, I told myself.

"Woof!" As if to instill courage in me, the ball of fur beside me barked.

"Graaah!" And as if in response, Gallus kicked off from the ground. He sprinted toward us, and the Sacred Beast rushed to meet him.

He's going to cut around and launch a slashing attack at the Sacred Beast from below. I could see it. If I used my stone cannon... No, the Sacred Beast was in my line of trajectory. I needed to use a different spell. What to use? The newbie told me to draw his attention, so...

"Explosion!"

"Gaaah!"

Just as the Sacred Beast sprang at Gallus, I conjured a small explosion right in front of his eyes.

"Not good enough!" Gallus drove all the weight of his body to the ground and rolled. He managed to slip right out from under the Sacred Beast, and after one roll, began to stand...

Just as he begins to stand, he's going to slash at me from down low.

"Ha!"

I stepped back to evade the attack. That was close. If I didn't have the Eye of Foresight, I would've died instantly.

"Tsk, so you're going to avoid that one!" Gallus shouted as he charged forward again, whipping his blade through the air.

He's going to slice at my abdomen from the side, then use that momentum for a return slash.

If I could see it, I could dodge it. He was faster than Eris, but he didn't have that unique rhythm of hers that was so difficult to read. There were no openings for me to launch a counterattack, but I saw the Sacred Beast getting back up in the periphery of my vision, so he could come bite Gallus from behind.

He's going to suddenly change his sword-wielding hand, then twist his body and leap upward.

For a moment I didn't understand that. I didn't understand what Gallus' movements meant.

"Gah...!"

Out of reflex, I stepped to the side instead of stepping backward. By the time I realized what was happening, his short sword came at me from straight above and drove right through the top of my foot. Even through the intense pain that shot through my body, I could see what was going to happen next.

Gallus is brandishing his sword, ready to swing.

My brain slowly worked out just what had happened. It was his foot—he'd hurled that short sword at me with his foot. Most likely an attack built into his boot! Being able to see into the future didn't help me at all with an opponent like this. I should have known better!

"It's over, Kennel Master!"

"Graaah!" The Sacred Beast leaped in and sunk its teeth into Gallus' shoulder.

"Gwah! You little...!"

"Yelp!" The pup screeched as it was flicked off, smashing hard into a tree.

In the lag of that moment, I channeled mana into my hand and launched a stone cannon.

"Tsk!"

My spell flew toward him at top speed, but Gallus just

split it in two in mid-air. Sparks erupted from the blade as it broke free from Gallus' hand. Good, now I could use this opportunity to pry the short sword from my—

Gallus is going to pick up the sword at his feet, and that'll be the end of it.

Oh no. That's when I realized that at some point he'd managed to back me into the place where the bodies of those beastmen were. The blade at his feet belonged to them. He'd led me here.

"I told you it was the end. Stop struggling, Kennel Master!"

I channeled mana between both my hands, betting my last hopes on this. Time seemed to slow. Gallus took a stance with his sword lowered toward his hips, about to unleash his attack. Even if I unleashed a shockwave to put distance between us, it was already too late. Instead of using stone cannon before, I would have been better off yanking the knife out of my foot or using the shockwave then. I'd made the wrong move.

"A North God Style original, Crying Bomb!" Just then, I heard the newbie's voice call out from behind me. Something suddenly went flying over my head—a black bag? And as it did, my vision of Gallus blurred.

Gallus will move to cut the bag full of powder in half but then will hesitate and cover his face with both arms instead.

The bag plopped against Gallus' face. An ash-like sub-stance exploded from it. Something to blind him, I guessed. But unfortunately, it failed... Wait, no, he was open!

In that moment I finished my spell and triggered a fiery explosion in the space between us. My body was thrown backward at a ridiculous speed. For just a split second, my consciousness left me.

I endured the pain that wracked my body and my foot alike and forced myself back up. The wound on my foot was...fine. Apparently the impact had wrenched the knife free. All of my toes were still intact. I could use healing magic to recover from this. To be honest, it hurt enough that I couldn't walk, but this was no time to be whining. I needed to stand right now and fight. The battle still wasn't over.

"Huh...?"

Gallus was already on the ground, lying face-up. His body didn't even twitch.

"...Woo-hoo! We did it!" When I glanced sideways, I saw Geese with his fist in the air. "The moment those North God Style guys hear the name 'Crying Bomb' they always use both hands to cover their face!"

I had no idea what that meant, but apparently those trained in the North God Style had some weird habit. Regardless, I approached Gallus with great caution.

"Hey, boss, be careful!"

Just as the newbie advised, I kept my guard up as I surveyed our unconscious opponent. I picked up his sword, which he had dropped nearby, and chucked it away. When I did, the Sacred Beast leaped into the air and caught the sword in its mouth before returning to me, tail wagging vigorously.

Yes, yes, you're a good boy, I thought. *But let's play frisbee another time, okay?*

"Newbie, take this." I patted the pup on the head a few times before tossing the sword over to Geese. Then I picked up a stick and started to prod at Gallus with it.

He didn't move. Even prodding around his eyes didn't get a flinch out of him. I bound his hands and legs and fastened a gag in his mouth, but his eyes remained shut. It seemed he was completely unconscious.

"We won." As the words tumbled out of my mouth, the Sacred Beast whined and Geese, who had removed the bag from the hostage's head, laughed. Had we really won? I was still basking in the afterglow of victory when the hostage child woke and began sobbing. Shortly after that, the beastfolk warriors finally arrived.

This had been quite the unique kidnapping case. It was a large-scale operation that the smuggling organization had plotted. They planned to steal the Sacred Beast, the Doldia's guardian deity. Their exact motivations were unclear, but apparently many people desired the Sacred Beast because of how special it was.

That said, even the simple act of kidnapping the Beast would prove challenging. Assuming they did manage it, the beastfolk, with their advanced sense of smell, would be hot on the smugglers' trail and immediately recapture the Beast. That's why the organization executed their plan around the rainy season.

The rainy season lasted three months. Each settlement busied itself with preparations, and warriors from each village had their hands tied. That said, it was impossible to sail a ship in the middle of the rainy season. So right before the rains began, they would steal the Beast and carry it off to the Demon Continent. That way they could get away with it easily and the warriors couldn't give pursuit.

The beastfolk were, of course, vigilant. During the preparations for the rainy season, children were forbidden from going outside and even the adults were cautious. It went without saying that the Sacred Beast was also well-guarded during that time. The organization took this into consideration as well.

First they employed every kidnapper in the area, and then they waited patiently. When the right time came, they raided each village and simultaneously abducted women and children. That's when the warriors panicked. The organization had intentionally hired those people to lower the kidnappings during the year so the beast-folk tribes would consequently lower their guard. Then, in one fell swoop, the smugglers kidnapped women and children from various settlements.

They also sent groups of armed forces they had prepared to strike those villages, but left the Doldia tribe's village untouched. Since this meant the Doldia's warriors were unoccupied, the other villages demanded assistance. The Doldia had to divide their forces to deliver aid to the various settlements.

As a result, the Doldia's village defenders were left shorthanded. That's when the smuggling organization used its elite forces to attack. They succeeded in abducting not only the tribal chief's granddaughter, but the Sacred Beast as well. It was a blitzkrieg tactic where minor forces distracted other settlements while the main force achieved their true objective.

The attack of armed forces, the kidnapping of children, and the kidnapping of the Sacred Beast... With all of that, it didn't matter how exceptional the beastfolk warriors were if there weren't enough of them. The tribal chief, Gustav, decided to abandon the children. He gathered his warriors and bolstered the village's defenses, then commenced a search for the Sacred Beast. The Beast was an important symbol to their village.

It seemed to them pure luck that they discovered the smugglers' holding area. They got a solid tip, and marched on the building in question. For now, let's just ignore that the source of this information was a separate force spearheaded by Gallus.

This was where the story I didn't know began: a story of what Ruijerd did in the intervening week when he left me in that cell.

Apparently Ruijerd became openly angry at the smugglers when he heard about what led to all of this. He proposed attacking their ship before it departed from the harbor. Gustav, however, disapproved. "We don't know which ship the children are on, and they know how to suppress our sense of smell."

That's exactly where Ruijerd came in. He proudly said he could use the crystal on his forehead to seek them out. As for Eris, she didn't participate as she had taken it upon herself to guard the children. With a great big grin on her face, I might add. That was certainly her Greyrat blood at play.

Anyway, Ruijerd's attack proved successful. Tragically for the smugglers, he discovered their ship and captured them only after beating them all half to death. The children came shuffling out from the depths of the ship. There were at least fifty of them. Everyone was saved and it was a nice happy ending, yay! ...Not.

Zant Port officials claimed it was an attack on the final voyage from that port before the rainy season began. There were important goods stored on that ship and attacking it was a serious felony.

Gustav, of course, protested this. The kidnapping and enslavement of beastfolk was a crime as far as the Holy Country of Millis and the tribal leaders of the Great Forest were concerned. Being punished for stopping that on their own shores seemed bizarre, he said. That only incensed the Zant Port officials. They insisted that they should have been informed ahead of time. But they'd just subdued the smugglers in the nick of time. They had no time to explain anything. Plus, there were fifty victims. Not five, not ten, *fifty* children! One or two were kidnapped from each settlement. Zant Port officials hadn't noticed any of it. In fact, some of the officials had taken bribes to pretend they knew nothing.

That was a violation of the treaty. If left as-is, it would create a huge fissure in the relationship between the beastfolk and the Holy Country of Millis. In the worst-case scenario, war would ensue. That's how dire the conversation became. At Gustav's command, the warriors were called to Zant Port and they stood at the entrance to the city in a standoff with its garrison.

In the end, Zant Port backed down. They paid the beastfolk a hefty sum in compensation. It took about a week for those negotiations to conclude and for the children to be returned to their parents. That was why I was left there for a week in that cell, to be dealt with last.

Well, not like there was any other choice. In fact, I thought it was amazing they managed to accomplish that much in just a week.

That's where Gallus took advantage of the situation. The Doldia's village defenses were weakened when Gyes called their band of warriors to Zant Port. Accompanied by his troops, Gallus stormed the settlement. He did this for the exact reason he'd mentioned before. He and those comrades he trusted would kidnap the children, and then he would be the one to make a profit.

Gallus targeted the period right before the rainy season began. He prepared for it by threatening the leader of the shipwrights into secretly building him a single ship. He must have been planning this for a while. Things had not happened exactly as he anticipated, but close enough for him to act. Sadly for him, his ambitions were left unfulfilled. In the end, his plan failed and he was handed off to the Zant Port officials. Thus the matter was resolved, and we had our happy ending.

CHAPTER 9
Slow Life in the Doldia Village

W E WERE WELCOMED into the Doldia village as heroes for saving the children and protecting the village against Gallus' attack. They wanted us to spend the rainy season living with them.

Gyes also officially apologized to me for ignoring orders, stripping me naked, and throwing me into a cell. And also for the freezing cold water that was thrown on me. It turned out that the beastfolk's unique way of kowtowing was lying face up with your stomach exposed. At first I thought he was making fun of me, but everyone present was dead serious about it. The only thing in my mind was jealousy as I stared at his hairy, muscular sixpack, so I just hurriedly accepted the apology.

Eris, however, did not. She was pissed when she learned what I had gone through and delivered a Boreas

Punch to Gyes' exposed belly before pouring water over his head. Once he looked like a drowned rat, she glared down at him and said, "Now we're even."

Eris never failed to impress me.

At the moment, we were in Gustav's house. It was the largest in the village, sitting well above the ground amongst the trees. Three stories tall and constructed of wood, it looked like it would collapse instantly in an earthquake, yet it was sturdy enough that an adult running around inside would cause not a single tremor.

There were eight of us here: Eris, Ruijerd and myself, as well as the Doldia tribal leader Gustav and his son Gyes, the leader of the warriors. One of the girls I'd rescued from the smugglers, Gyes' middle daughter, Minitona, was also present. His oldest daughter, Linianna, was apparently off studying in a different country. And then there was another girl we had rescued who was of the Adoldia tribe: the Adoldia tribal leader's middle daughter, Tersena. She was a dog-eared girl who was quite well-developed for her age. She had been planning to return home, but that was disrupted when the rainy season began, and she would be spending the next three months here.

The girls were talking animatedly, with woofs and mews, about how they had almost been kidnapped. "I'm so glad I didn't get abducted. I heard there's a sick, twisted noble family in Asura that's only sexually interested in beastfolk. Who knows what would have happened to me."

Gallus also talked about how a certain noble family paid especially well for beastfolk with Doldia blood. Those who were easy to train, it seemed, sold for the highest prices.

"There's no place among Asuran nobles for that kind of scum!" And there was Eris, talking as if this conversation had nothing to do with her or her family, even though it was really likely that said noble family had a certain rodent-ish name. One that started with the letter G.

I never asked where the maids in Eris' household came from, but perhaps some of them had been kidnapped. Eris' grandfather, Sauros, was a good man, but his world-view had odd aspects to it. Well, I would keep my mouth shut. Some things were better left unsaid.

Eris seemed to remember something because she suddenly showed them the ring on her finger. "By the way, do you know Ghislaine? This ring here belongs to her." Eris didn't know the Beast God tongue, so she spoke to them in them in the human tongue. Of those present, the only ones who could understand the language other than Ruijerd and myself were Gustav and Gyes.

"Ghislaine...?" Gyes' face puckered. "She's...still alive?"

"Huh?"

His voice filled with disgust. He spat out the words as if they left a bitter taste on his tongue. "She's a stain on our tribe."

That was only the beginning of Gyes bashing on Ghislaine. He spoke in the tongue of men so Eris could understand. His voice was full of emotion unfit for an older brother speaking of his younger sister, as he went on and on about what a mistake Ghislaine was as a person.

It was difficult for me to listen to it all, given that Ghislaine had once saved my life. It seemed she had done some truly despicable things in the village, but still, this all happened when she was a child. The Ghislaine I knew was clumsy, but hardworking. She'd changed, readjusted herself as a person. She didn't deserve to be spoken of like this. She was a highly respectable sword instructor as well as an accomplished apprentice of magic.

So, I thought, *how should I put this nicely...? Knock it off.*

"That ring too, that was something our mother gave her so she'd stop going berserk without reason. Not that it ever did any good. She was just a destructive good-for-nothing."

"You—" I started to say.

"Oh, shut up! What do you even know about Ghislaine?!" Eris cut me off, bellowing in a voice loud enough to split the house in two. The others were left dumbfounded by her outburst. After all, only Gyes and Gustav could understand the language.

I was afraid Eris might turn violent. But instead she looked frustrated, tears welling in her eyes. She balled her hands into trembling fists, but she didn't swing them.

"Ghislaine is amazing! Amazingly amazing! If you call for help, she'll come immediately! She's super fast! And super strong!" Words that Eris probably wasn't even thinking about spilled from her mouth. Even though the others didn't understand what she was saying, the sorrow in her voice conveyed the meaning well enough. And she was also expressing my emotions.

"Ghislaine is...hic...guh...not someone you can just... hic..." Eris tried her best to not punch anyone, even through her tears.

That's right, she couldn't punch Gyes here. Ghislaine had been violent during her time in this village. If Eris swung a fist here, Gyes could just say, "See? They're two peas in a pod."

When I looked over at Gyes, he seemed confused. "No, I can't... This is unbelievable. Ghislaine...is respected? This can't..."

Seeing that, I tamped my anger down. "Let's stop this conversation here," I suggested, putting my arms around Eris' shoulders.

Eris looked at me in disbelief. "Why... Rudeus, do you...hate Ghislaine?"

"No, I like Ghislaine too. The person we know and the person they know may share the same name, but she's a different person." I looked at Gyes. Even he would reconsider his stance if he met Ghislaine now. Time changed people. I knew that first-hand.

"...Fine." Eris didn't seem satisfied, but at least she seemed relieved by what I said.

"Wait, is she—is Ghislaine really such an incredible person now?"

"I respect her, at the very least."

My words drove Gyes into deep contemplation. Considering what we'd heard him say, there must have been a lot that happened between him and Ghislaine. He boiled with anger at the mere mention of her. Being related by blood made it worse.

"So, could you apologize to us?"

"...My apologies."

The atmosphere became a bit uneasy after that. Perhaps because it was the second time we'd forced Gyes to apologize to us that day.

As for Ghislaine, I'd completely forgotten about her this past year, but she'd probably been displaced during the incident as well. I wondered where she was and what she was doing. Knowing her, I figured she was probably searching for Eris and me. It was frustrating that we were unable to gather any information during our time in Zant Port.

One week passed. Rain continued falling the entire time. We were given an empty house in the village and spent our time there. We were given food regardless of whether or not we contributed anything since we were considered heroes of the Great Forest, even though the village was in dire straits after the damage from the fire.

The land was flooded, and chaos erupted when a child fell into the water. People were quite shocked but grateful when I used my magic to save them. I thought perhaps I should use my magic to blow away the rainclouds, but I gave up on that thought quickly. Roxy said it herself: Manipulating the weather wasn't a good idea. If I forced the rain to stop, something awful might happen to the woods.

To be honest, I just wanted it to hurry up and stop so we could move on. But then again, it was supposed to stop after three months. I just had to bear with it until then.

It was raining when I decided to take a stroll through the village. Given that it was just a village, there was no weaponsmith, armorer or inn of any type. For the most part it was private housing and storehouses, or guardhouses for their warriors. All of this was built above the trees.

This village was the real thing, in 3-D! Truly fascinating. My heart thrummed in excitement just walking around. There was one spot where you weren't allowed to proceed any further. Apparently there was a special place beyond that point. I had no intentions of intruding upon it.

During my walk, I came upon a pathway that intersected on two levels. I waited on the lower one hoping that a girl might pass by above me, but it was Geese who crossed it.

"Yo, newbie! So you got out too, eh?"

He looked happy and waved at me. He'd also received amnesty for his contributions when the village was in trouble. "Yup. 'Never do it again,' they said. Morons, all of them. Of course I'm going to do it again."

"Hey everyone! Did you hear that? This guy hasn't learned his lesson!"

"Hey now! Come on, knock it off. I can't run off right now, not until the rainy season is over."

In other words, he *was* planning to repeat his mistake. Honestly, what a hopeless case. "Also, allow me to return your vest."

"I told you to knock off that polite crap. Just take the vest," he said.

"Are you sure?"

"It's still cold out during this season."

Still, he didn't seem like a totally bad guy at least. The way he was kind and yet noncommittal reminded me of Paul. Paul... I wondered if he was doing well.

Two weeks passed, and the rain wasn't stopping.

I learned that the Doldia had their own secret magic. It allowed them to find enemies by using a far-reaching howl, and with their special voices, they could make opponents lose their sense of balance. The way Gyes paralyzed me with his voice was one of those types of magic. From what I heard, it seemed to be a magic that manipulated sound.

When I told Gustav "I'd love for you to teach me," he heartily agreed. Unfortunately, no matter how many times he demonstrated it for me, I couldn't imitate it perfectly. It seemed the magic depended on the unique vocal cords of the Doldia.

Of course it does, I thought bitterly to myself. In all likelihood I couldn't use most of the unique magic that individual tribes possessed. It seemed unfair that beast-folk and other races could use human magic so easily. I knew the key element was to channel mana into my voice, but no matter how I did it, the result was always subpar. The best I could do was make my opponent flinch for a moment. It seemed I would be no Wagan, after all.

On that note, Gustav was quite shocked at how I used magic without chanting. "Do the magic schools these days teach that, too?"

"It's because my master taught me so well," I explained, praising Roxy for no apparent reason.

"Oh? And where's your master from?"

"The Migurd tribe, from the Demon Continent's Biegoya Region. Her magic... I think she learned from the Academy of Magic?"

When I told Gustav that I also planned to go to the Academy of Magic, he seemed impressed and said, "Wow, you're already at that level and yet you're still motivated to improve?" That made me feel good.

Three weeks passed.

Monsters appeared in this village as well. One was a water strider, surfing swiftly across the water below only to leap up suddenly and attack. Another was like a water snake which slid its way up along the trees. The village was guarded by its band of warrior beastfolk, but their impressive noses and sonar-like voices were no use in the rain, so often monsters would slip by their watchful gaze and infest the village.

As Eris and I were walking around, one of the beastfolk children nearly got snatched up by a chameleon-like reptile right before us. I promptly shot it down with my stone cannon, and the child adorably wagged their tail and thanked me.

I was strangely popular among the children in this village, no doubt because I was the hero who saved them in their time of need. Occasionally they would come up to me and lick me on the cheek or show me the collection of acorns they'd gathered before the rainy season hit. I was practically a celebrity.

Eris, in a true display of her family's infamy, couldn't contain her excitement when she saw such a huge gathering of so many adorable children with ears and tails. She annoyed the children by breathing erratically as she patted their heads and touched their tails.

We couldn't just stand by while such adorable creatures were attacked by monsters. That was why I proposed that Ruijerd help with the village's defenses, but he opposed the idea.

"The warriors here take pride in their role in the village," he said. Protecting this village was their duty. As long as they didn't request the aid of an outsider, it wasn't our business to intrude. That was Ruijerd's belief, anyway. I didn't understand it at all.

"But isn't the children's safety more important than that?"

Ruijerd paused and thought for a few seconds before turning to Gyes for his input.

Gyes welcomed the idea. "Oh, Master Ruijerd, you're going to lend us your assistance? That would be a big help!" The kidnapping incident had dramatically decreased the number of their warriors. So Gyes offered to compensate Ruijerd for his assistance on behalf of the warrior band.

That was how all the monsters in the village were exterminated. Ruijerd would find them and I would use my magic to defeat them. We would retrieve their bodies, strip them of useful materials and sell them to Gyes. It was a beneficial cycle.

Ruijerd was right about one thing. The village's warriors disapproved of us at first. It wasn't until we mercilessly annihilated any monster that entered the village and they realized the rainy season would pass without any casualties that they finally broke into smiles.

"I thought their tribe had more pride than this. It's disgraceful, entrusting the protection of their village to another race." Ruijerd was the only one bothered by this. It seemed the beastfolk of several hundred years ago were quite different from their modern counterparts.

One month passed.

The strength of the downpour seemed to be waning, but that was probably just my imagination. Eris, Minitona, and Tersena were becoming fast friends. They seemed to enjoy traveling around together despite the rain. I wondered what they were doing.

It turns out Eris was teaching them the Human tongue. Yes, you heard me. Eris was teaching other people a language! This wasn't the time or place for me to barge in and try to help her; I'd only destroy her image. I was a man who could read the room, after all.

This was the first time Eris had friends her own age. It made me proud seeing her getting along so well with the girls. The red hair, the cat ears, and the dog ears... Seeing them all happily romping around was more than enough for me.

Although Eris should be careful about thoughtlessly wrapping her arms around them like that. They might misunderstand her intentions, just like they did with me. In fact, Mister Gyes was watching. How would he feel as a parent, seeing Eris with her nostrils flared, throwing her arms around his daughter?

"Ah, Lady Eris, I appreciate you getting along so well with my daughter."

What the—? This was a totally different reaction from the one he gave me! He should've been able to smell the excitement radiating off of Eris right now, so why didn't he? That was just the difference between men and women, I guessed. Yeah, that had to be it. Of course it was.

"By the way, I am very sorry about the matter with Ghislaine. We haven't seen one another in a very long time, so perhaps I've misunderstood her. It seems my younger sister has grown a bit during her time in the world." He bowed his head. It seemed he'd come to terms with that in the past month. That was good.

"Of course she has. She's Sword King Ghislaine! And you know what else? Ghislaine can use magic now, too," Eris boasted.

"Hahaha, Ghislaine using magic? Lady Eris, your jokes are very clever."

"Seriously," Eris insisted. "Rudeus taught her reading, arithmetic, and magic."

"Lord Rudeus did...?"

After that, Eris began fiercely boasting about Ghislaine and me. She talked about my lessons back in the Fittoa Region. She started with how poorly she and Ghislaine had been at learning, and how much she respected me for sticking with both of them and teaching them all the way till the end. I felt embarrassed listening to it.

Gyes said how impressed he was again and again, and when the three finally parted, he came over to the wooden box I had hidden in to eavesdrop. "So tell me, what's a respectable teacher doing in a place like this?"

"O-observing people is a hobby of mine," I stammered.

"Ah, yes, that seems like a very noble hobby to have. By the way, how did you teach Ghislaine how to read?"

"Nothing special, really. I just did it the normal way."

"The normal way...? I can't picture it," Gyes said.

"When she was an adventurer, she went through a lot

of hardship because she wasn't educated. It makes sense that you wouldn't be able to picture it."

"So that's the story. When she was little, my sister was never happy unless she could hit someone when something happened that she didn't like."

Judging from what he was saying, Ghislaine sounded like she was just like Eris when she was a young girl. Specifically, the parts where she would pick fights with people and that, because she was strong, few could stop her. Gyes must have gotten himself burned by that fire numerous times. He wasn't a very good older brother if he was that much weaker than his little sister.

Speaking of older brothers, I was one too. I wondered if Norn and Aisha were doing well. I'd been wanting to write a letter to them, but I kept forgetting. Once the rain stopped, we would head for the capital of the Holy Country of Millis, and there I would send a letter to Buena Village. If I had sent one from the Demon Continent it probably wouldn't have made it, but surely it would have no trouble if I sent it from Millis.

"By the way, Master Rudeus."

"Yes?"

"Just how long do you plan to stay inside that wooden box?"

Until they came in here to get changed, of course. It was almost nighttime, after all. Right now they were going to go play in the water, but then they would have to change into their nightclothes afterward.

"Sniff, sniff... I can smell the sexual excitement on you."

"Whaat?! No way; that's absurd. Perhaps somewhere there's a certain beastfolk-loving girl looking ecstatic now that she's relieved herself?"

As I tried to play dumb, Gyes' eyebrow twitched. "Master Rudeus. I am grateful for what you did before. I am also apologetic, even now, for having misunderstood you." His tone took a sudden shift. "But if you put your hand on my daughter, it'll be a completely different story. If you don't get out of that box right now, I'm going to throw it into the floodwaters."

He was serious. I didn't hesitate. I leaped out of that box in a flash, at the same speed of one of those Tomy Pop-up Pirates.

"I'm a protector of this village. I don't want to have to say this to you but...restrain yourself a little."

"Yes, sir."

Yeah, well, I *did* get a little too carried away. That I would admit.

A month and a half passed.

Ruijerd and Gustav got along like a house on fire. Ruijerd paid frequent visits to the Dedoldia house, and the two drank together and swapped tales of their pasts. The stories were packed with gore, but they were actually pretty interesting to listen to. Almost like listening to an ex-biker gang member exaggerate about what a badass he was in his younger days. Except the things Ruijerd and Gustav said probably did actually happen.

Thanks to those conversations, I got a better understanding of the beastfolk. "Beastfolk" was a generic term for the tribes that lived in the Great Forest. There were many that originated here but crossed over to the Demon Continent and came to be referred to as demons. An outward characteristic of these tribes was that one part of their body retained an animal-like appearance. Each tribe also had one of five senses enhanced. In a broad sense, Nokopara and Blaze were also once a part of the beastfolk.

The Doldia were particularly special among the tribes of beastfolk. Only one tribe maintained the peace of the forest while also protecting the Sacred Beast. That was the Doldia.

Then there were the cat-like Dedoldia and the dog-like Adoldia. Those were the two primary families that were

divided into a dozen branch families. In other words, the
royalty of the Great Forest. Although they weren't doing
much to deserve the title, they were the ones who would
lead when the necessity arose.

There were also elves and hobbits living in the Great
Forest. They were concentrated in the northern part
of the forest, so they didn't have much contact with
the beastfolk. However, all the tribes would gather for
a meeting once a year, and they would participate in a
festival near the Great Sacred Tree. According to Gustav,
while their tribes had differences, they all lived as friends
in the Great Forest.

As for the dwarves, they lived not in the Great
Forest but farther south, at the foot of the Blue Wyrm
Mountains. The blue dragons flew across the world and
only returned to the mountain range to nest when they
were laying eggs or raising their young, like migratory
birds. Unlike migratory birds, however, they only returned once every ten years.

Since time immemorial, men and beastfolk had
cycled through war and friendship with one another.
One war, which was really more of a small competition,
took place just fifty years ago. Gustav regaled us with
stories of his involvement, and how the beastfolk's strongest band of warriors mowed down a group of human

soldiers that had wandered into the forest. It was quite overdramatized, but hearing the way things played out from the beastfolk's point of view was quite fresh and entertaining.

To counter this, Ruijerd whipped out his trump card, the story about the Superd Clan during Laplace's War. The two traded banter as if they were competing, but given that they were both old men, it more or less turned into a sermon about the good old days.

"Warriors these days are a complete disgrace."

"I understand what you mean completely, Master Ruijerd. Many of them are feeble and weak."

"Exactly," Ruijerd said. "Men in my youth were tough and strong."

Literally kindred spirits. This might have been a different world from my first, but the camaraderie of old men sure was the same.

"You're precisely right. Gyes may lead the warriors now, but he lacks judgment. He's good at leading people, but if he could assess situations better, then Master Rudeus wouldn't have gone through all of that," Gustav said.

Ruijerd disagreed. "No, Rudeus is a warrior. He should have understood that if he let his guard down in enemy territory, he ran the risk of being caught and held as a captive. Yet he still let his guard down. If he'd taken things seriously, he would have been able to best someone like Gyes. That was his own failure."

Ouch. As true as it was, that hurt. Ruijerd had faith in me, which was why he allowed me to go alone. Yet I was caught so easily. In a way, I'd betrayed his trust.

"But Master Ruijerd, isn't that a bit heartless? Your comrade had something terrible happen to him."

"As a warrior, you must take responsibility for your own battles. Besides, Rudeus could have escaped on his own at any point. I appreciate that he trusts me as his companion, but he's not a child. A warrior doesn't force their comrades into a difficult position by allowing themselves to get caught!"

Boy, Ruijerd, you sure are hammered, I thought. *Maybe you could escape on your own if you got caught, but try not to expect too much out of me. My powers aren't limitless, okay?*

Two months passed.

Whenever I was in my room, the Sacred Beast would come plodding in. The beast lived deeper in the village alongside the flowers and the butterflies, but once a day during its walk time it would roam about the village freely. Its favorite (and current) route was wherever I was.

"Well, if it isn't the Sacred Beast. What business do you have here with a sex fiend like me?"

"Ruff!"

"Life's *ruff*, huh?"

"Ruff!"

That wasn't much of an answer.

I wasn't sure whether the Sacred Beast was male or female, but either way it settled down beside me. At the moment I was holding the beginnings of a figurine in my hands. It looked like it would be some time before the rain stopped, so I decided to try making one.

It was modeled after Ruijerd. You might be wondering why I picked him, but just think about it. The Superd were faceless boogeymen. People trembled with fear when they saw green hair, but there was no color on the figure I made. It was just a completely ash-gray stone figure. Perhaps if it was impressive enough, people might become more accepting of him.

First was the silhouette. The hair would come last.

"Woof." The Sacred Beast pressed its body against my thigh and rested its head atop my knee. I was puzzled, given that I'd never had an animal come up to me like this before.

"Arf?" It looked at my hands as if to ask what I was doing. The pup was quite calm despite its young age.

I finally settled on stroking its neck. "I don't have anything else to do, so I'm creating something."

"Woof." The beast licked my hand and wagged its tail. Clearly it didn't hate me. It was still raining outside, so it probably didn't have anything else to do, either. It was probably yearning for some excitement.

"Want to play?"

"Woof!"

So the two of us grappled and roughhoused. I got to enjoy its soft fluffy fur, and the Sacred Beast received a moderate amount of exercise. Truly a win-win situation.

Knock, knock. Someone was rapping on the door as we were in the midst of playing.

"Hm? Come on in."

"Pardon me." A woman in warrior's dress came in. It was Laklana. She was one of those in charge of the Sacred Beast, and she would come retrieve it when its walk time was near an end.

"Nice to see you again."

"You as well, Master Rudeus. Also, about that time before..." Every time she saw me, Laklana would apologize for the time when she threw freezing cold water on me. The first apology had been more than enough. "That aside, could you please stop being so attached to the Sacred Beast?"

"What are you talking about? I'm just having fun playing with it."

What, was this another false accusation? She really didn't feel sorry about anything, did she? If she wasn't careful with her words, next time she would be the one naked in a jail cell and I would be the one pouring the water.

"But I can smell your arousal."

"...It's not for the reason you're thinking."

The real reason was because every time she came and bowed her head, my inner pervert began to whisper, "*Hey lady, if you could solve this with a simple sorry, we wouldn't need to call the cops, now would we? If you really want to solve this, you know what you gotta do, right? Let's take it to the bedroom together.*"

"The Sacred Beast is extremely precious to the Doldia. I'm aware that you saved it from harm, but developing feelings for it is—"

"Except I don't have any feelings for it."

The Sacred Beast was a type of magical beast born once every few hundred years. It didn't have a proper name. Since ages long past, it only appeared when the world faced a crisis, and when it became an adult it would set out alongside a hero, using its great power to save the world.

That was how the legend went, anyway. That was why the Sacred Beast was raised with such immense care, deep within the Doldia Village, in a restricted area where there stood a great tree they called the Sacred Tree. So of course it had lived a sheltered life. They were careful not to expose the pup to the outside world, which it knew little about. It was still a dog, though, so they allowed it time for a walk once daily.

It would apparently take another hundred years before the Sacred Beast reached adulthood. If the stories were true, the world would meet with calamity then. In the meantime, Laklana was overseeing the protection of the Sacred Beast. As for the Sacred Tree, it was located beyond that blocked-off path I had visited earlier.

"Could it be that...Lord Rudeus is the hero?"

"Woof!" The pup gave a bark.

Laklana's expression turned to shock. "What?! What are you saying?"

Hm? What was she talking about?

"Arf!"

"I see then, but—"

"Woof!"

"...I understand."

Why the heck are you talking to this dog as if you're having a normal conversation? I thought. I could hear it barking. That was definitely not the Beast God tongue. Just how was she understanding it? Was she using a Bow-Lingual translator?

"The Sacred Beast said that you're not the one."

"I figured as much." Although I wished she'd elaborate.

"But the Sacred Beast is very grateful to you, it seems."

"Oh? I was left in that cell the whole time, so I figured it forgot about me."

"Woof!"

"Regrettable, the Sacred Beast said, but it did ask us to feed you delicious food. Master Rudeus, you did enjoy the meals we provided you, yes?"

Indeed. The food at least was very good. I also received seconds when I asked for them. I did think that was strange for a jail. So the Sacred Beast had arranged that for me? Using food as a form of gratitude sounded exactly like something a dog would do.

"Although if you were going to do that, I would have preferred you release me from my cell, at least."

"Woof!" (Or apparently, "What's a cell?")

"A place where you lock up bad people," I explained.

"Arf! ('But I'm also locked up.')"

We continued for a bit after that, having a conversation with Laklana as our interpreter. It seemed the Sacred Beast didn't know all the details about what happened.

That included not being aware of the smell of arousal that Gyes claimed was coming off me, or why Gyes had then taken me into custody. It didn't seem to know much about the meaning of its kidnapping either, beyond that it was a terrifying experience. In other words, it was still just a child. It wasn't right to demand reparations from a child, so I gave up on that.

"I did get to live more comfortably because of you, so thank you." At my gratitude, it wagged its tail and licked my face.

Heh heh, you sure are a cute one, I thought as I stroked its neck, only to be pushed to the ground. *Aah, you can't! Not where people can see us...!*

"Master Rudeus, this is the Sacred Beast's way of showing respect. Could you please try to restrain your affections?"

"You're misunderstanding, what you're smelling is my arousal because of *you*."

"Huh?!"

"That was rude of me; disregard that." Crap, crap. I let my true feelings slip out.

"Ahem...Sacred Beast, it's time we returned to the Sacred Tree."

"Woof!"

The beast obediently turned to leave, just as it was told, and went without a single complaint.

This became a daily occurrence. But let's just keep it a secret between us that a few days later, Laklana got incredibly pissed at me when I tried to teach the Sacred Beast how to shake.

Just like that, with nothing terribly eventful occurring, three months passed and the rain stopped.

CHAPTER 10

The Holy Sword Highway

THE EVE BEFORE we left the Doldia Village, Eris and Minitona had a fight. It went without saying, I'm sure, but Eris won easily. Of course she did. She was able to keep up with Ruijerd's training, after all. When the other person was younger and had no training, they were hardly even an opponent. It was more like the strong bullying the weak.

I thought I should at least warn Eris about this. I knew she was that type of person, but she would soon be fourteen. While technically still a child, fourteen was old enough that she couldn't just indiscriminately punch another person. But just how was I going to word it?

I had never stopped one of Eris' fights before. Normally I left Ruijerd to deal with her and her quarrels in the Adventurers' Guild. So what could I even say at this point? Should I tell her that adventurers and village girls were different matters?

"N-no, it's Tona's fault," Tersena said in protest.

According to her, now that the rainy season was over, Eris had said she was going to leave the village and Minitona tried to stop her. Eris was happy that Minitona wanted her to stay, but she explained why she had to continue her journey, pointing out that Minitona's request was a selfish one. It was usually the other way around with Eris.

They continued talking for a while after that. At first the two of them were calm, but their dispute soon grew heated. Minitona began hurling insults. Among them were things about Ghislaine and myself. Eris looked annoyed, but endured it all and replied calmly.

In the end, Minitona threw the first punch. She was the one who tried to pick a fight with Eris. That took a lot of courage. I gave her props for that. It was definitely something I couldn't do. Eris didn't back down. As expected, she mercilessly beat Minitona to a pulp.

"Eris."

"What?!"

I stopped to reconsider the situation. Firstly, Minitona should have known she would lose the fight, yet she still got heated and started throwing insults. Even after she got pulverized by Eris, she still wouldn't back down. The best of adults broke easily when facing Eris. Minitona had to be quite strong-willed.

"You did hold back, didn't you?" I asked Eris.

"Of course I did," she said, turning from me. In the past, Eris would never have shown mercy to someone who bared their teeth at her, not even if they were a child. I knew that especially well.

"Normally you'd be meaner about things, wouldn't you?"

"Yeah, well, she's my friend."

When I looked at her, Eris looked ashamed, her lips pushed in a pout.

Hm. It seemed she did regret punching Minitona at least a little. That was something I'd never seen before. In three months, maybe she'd become a little bit more of an adult. She was maturing without me even noticing. In that case there was only one thing to say.

"You'd better make up with her before we leave tomorrow."

"...Don't want to."

Still a child, huh?

We were busy preparing for our departure on the last

day, so I didn't meet with the Sacred Beast. Instead I got two visitors in the middle of the night.

"Ah!" came a small cry accompanied by a loud crash.

Those two sounds were enough to wake me. I got up, aware of how much I'd lowered my guard lately, and reached for the staff at my side. Our intruder's aura was too pathetic to be a burglar. Ruijerd would have noticed one long before they got this far, anyway. That made the intruder's silence all the more bizarre.

"Tersena, try to be a little more quiet, mew!"

I put down my staff. So that was why Ruijerd said nothing.

"Sorry, Tona, but it's dark."

"If you squint your eyes enough you can see, mew... Ah!"

Another sharp banging sound.

"Tona, are you okay?"

"Owie, mew..."

Perhaps the two of them were trying to whisper, but their voices were loud enough I could hear them clearly. Just what was their objective? Money? Fame? Or were they aiming for my body?

Kidding, of course. I knew it was Eris.

"Ah, here, mew?"

"Sniff, sniff... Nope, this doesn't seem to be her."

"Don't worry about it, mew. They're probably sleeping, mew."

The girls stopped in front of my door and I heard a click as they entered. Cautiously they peeked in and looked around, only to lock eyes with me as I sat up in my bed.

"Mew...!"

"What's wrong, Tona? Ah...!"

It was Minitona and Tersena. They were each wearing a thin leather dress with a gap over the rear where their wiggling tails peeked out. This sleepwear was peculiar to the beastfolk, and it was truly adorable.

I spoke as quietly as I could. "What are you doing here so late at night? Eris' room is next door."

"S-sorry, mew..." Tona apologized and started to shut the door before pausing suddenly. "That's right, I haven't thanked you yet, mew."

Huh, T-Tona?

Minitona spoke as if she'd just remembered and slipped inside the room. Tersena timidly followed her.

"Thank you for saving us, mew. I was told I might've died if you hadn't cast your healing on me, mew."

That was probably true. Her wounds were quite serious. At least severe enough that I would've been pretty traumatized in her place. I thought her undaunted attitude was impressive.

"Not a problem," I said.

"Thanks to you, I don't have any scars either, mew." She rolled up the hem of her dress, revealing her bare legs. It was just dark enough I couldn't see what was between them. Lady Kishirika, why didn't you have any demon eyes that could see in the dark?

"Tona, that's improper...!"

"It's not like he hasn't seen it before, so it's fine, mew."

"But Uncle Gyes said that human men have a long mating season, so if you don't approach them with caution you might get assaulted."

A long mating season? That was a rude thing to say. Not that it was wrong.

"Besides, if he gets that turned on from looking at my body, then it's a good way for me to say thanks... mew?! It's cold!"

"That's because you keep holding your dress up!"

At that point, I wasn't even focused on Minitona's legs. A cold sweat ran down my back as I curled my fingers around the staff that should have been lying at my side. A vicious, murderous intent oozed from the neighboring room.

"A-ahem. I'll accept your gratitude. Eris is in the room beside mine, so go on."

That's right, it didn't matter if she was a child. She shouldn't have been carelessly showing off her body like that. It would cause real problems if she were assaulted by some sick old man trying to play doctor, after all.

"Okay. But really, thank you, mew."

"Thank you," Tersena chimed. The two of them bowed and left the room.

After a few moments I tiptoed across the room and put my ear to the wall. I could hear Eris' sullen voice in the neighboring room as she said, "What do you want?"

I pictured her in her usual pose, arms folded over her chest. Minitona's and Tersena's voices were a bit difficult to hear. Or maybe Eris' voice was just too loud. I listened anxiously, but Eris' voice gradually grew calmer. It seemed like things would be okay. Relieved, I returned to my bed.

The three girls spent the entire night talking. As for what they talked about, I had no idea. Minitona and Tersena were far from being masters of the human tongue. Eris had learned a little of the Beast tongue, but not enough to hold a conversation. I worried whether they'd really sorted things out or not, but when it was time to part the next day, Eris held Minitona's hand and had tears in their eyes when they hugged. It seemed they were able to make up after all. I was glad.

The Holy Sword Highway was a road that went straight through the Great Forest. Built long ago by the Holy Country of Millis, it was bursting with mana. Even as the area around it flooded, the highway remained dry and untouched. Apparently no monster would set foot on it. The three of us would be using the horse-drawn carriage we'd gotten from the Doldia tribe to travel down that road, heading south.

The beastfolk prepared everything we could possibly need for our trip. The carriage, the horse, travel money, and supplies. We could head straight to the capital of Millis without once returning to Zant Port.

It was time to head out! Or at least it was supposed to be, when for some reason a monkey-faced man approached us.

"Oh man, this is perfect timing. I was just thinking about going back to Millis. Let me ride with you guys," Geese said, shamelessly hauling himself inside.

"Oh, it's you, Geese."

"You're coming along, too?"

The other two didn't sound as annoyed by his appearance as I did. When I asked if they knew him, their answer showed he'd been gradually warming up to them without me noticing. This included cozying up to Eris, Minitona, and Tersena, and sharing amusing anecdotes.

He'd also joined Gustav and Ruijerd during their chats, where Geese adjusted his manner to fit the tone of the conversation. He truly was a smooth talker and skilled at manipulation. He managed to successfully ingratiate himself with both of them without me noticing a thing. And the two of them had just welcomed him so easily. What, were they cheating on me with Geese?!

"All right then, let's get going!" Ruijerd declared as the carriage lurched into motion.

We waved farewell to the beastfolk who gathered to see us off. It was a bit moving to see Eris with tears in her eyes as she watched Minitona and the others.

Still, something heavy weighed on my heart, and it was entirely Geese's fault. If he wanted to tag along, he should have said so in the first place. There was no need for him to act so shady and sneak around behind my back. I wouldn't have refused him if he'd flat-out asked me. After we'd eaten the same food and picked off each other's fleas, it felt distancing.

"Hey, hey, boss. Don't glare at me like that. We're friends, right?"

Geese must have noticed the disgruntled look I no doubt had as we sat in the coach, blazing down the road at an impressive speed. He grinned at me and leaned close to my ear.

"Might not look it, but I have confidence in my skills as a cook, just you watch!"

He had a charming face, and he wasn't a bad guy, either. Still, ever since the incident with Gallus, I had a lingering sense that there was something darker behind all of that.

"Rudeus."

"Yes, Mister Ruijerd?"

"Who cares if he tags along?" he said.

"Master Ruijerd!" Geese exclaimed. "I knew you would understand! Ahh, it just confirms what I already thought about you. You truly are a man among men!"

"Are you sure about this, Mister Ruijerd?" I asked. "This man is one of those criminals that you loathe so much."

"He doesn't look that bad to me."

I had no idea what Ruijerd's metric for measuring that was. Geese coming along was fine, but Ruijerd's double standards were bad. No, perhaps this was all a result of Geese's smooth talk with him. The monkey bastard sure had done a good job.

"Heh heh. I do gamble, but I don't think I've ever done anything truly contemptible to another person. Master Ruijerd, you have a good eye for people."

Frankly, I did owe this man a debt. He gave me his vest when I was cold, and he helped me out during the fight with Gallus, too. I wasn't sure what he was planning, but

I had no reason to turn him away. I was just a bit irritated at his roundabout methods, that was all.

"I don't mind if you come with us, newbie. But are you sure you're not scared of a Superd?" I spoke loud enough that Ruijerd could hear. I wasn't sure yet if he knew the fact that Ruijerd was a Superd, but if he partook in their drinking festivities, he may very well have heard. I just didn't want him to find out later and complain about how terrifying it was being with a Superd.

"Of course. Did you think I wouldn't be? I am a demon, after all. I've been hearing about how scary the Superd are ever since I was a kid."

"Oh really? You know, Ruijerd may not look it right now, but he's a Superd."

When Geesc heard that, he narrowed his eyes. "That's different. He saved my life."

Curious as to what that meant, I turned my gaze to Ruijerd, but he only shook his head as if he had no idea what Geese was talking about. At the very least, it wasn't something that had occurred within these last three months.

"Guess you don't remember, huh? Well, it was thirty years ago, after all."

Geese then launched into an explanation. It was an epic story that included an initial meeting, a parting, a climax, and a love scene. When an incredibly handsome hard-boiled hero said he was going to set out on a journey, hundreds of women pleaded with him to not go. He set out from his hometown despite his lingering attachments to it and encountered a mysterious beauty when he arrived at his destination.

To summarize what would otherwise be a long tale, when Geese was still a novice adventurer, Ruijerd stepped in to save him when he was attacked and nearly killed by a monster.

"Well, it was thirty years ago. I don't particularly feel like I owe him for it or anything," Geese said. The Superd tribe was scary, but Ruijerd was different, the monkey-faced newbie said with a laugh.

Ruijerd relaxed when he heard that. I felt like I understood the meaning of the word *karma* after hearing that story. *Good for you, Ruijerd*, I thought.

"Well, I hope you'll let me stay with you for a while, Senpai~☆"

And that was how Dead End gained a new member in the form of a monkey-faced— Hang on now, he wasn't a new member. He was only staying with us until we reached the next city, I reminded myself. Geese claimed that he was jinxed—whenever he was in a party of four, something terrible happened. I had no words for how he managed to get thrown into a cell with me despite purposefully avoiding that jinx. In any case, it was fine if he wasn't going to join our party.

That was how we set off on our journey with an extra traveler accompanying us.

The carriage carried us along on a nonstop path that cut through the Great Forest. It really was a straight road, one that stretched unbroken into the horizon, continuing all the way to the Holy Country's capital. There wasn't a single monster, and water drained right off the road.

I was suspicious about how such a path came to be, but Geese explained for me. This highway was created by Saint Millis, the founder of the Millis faith, the biggest religious denomination in the world. With a single swipe of their sword, Saint Millis cut the mountains and the forests in half, splitting a demon king on the Demon Continent into two. The road was named the Holy Sword Highway with that story in mind.

As much as I wanted to skeptically dismiss the story, Saint Millis' mana still remained. The fact that we had encountered no monsters thus far was proof of that.

The carriage hadn't gotten stuck in any mud, either. We were sailing along smoothly. It was nothing short of a miracle.

I could understand now why their religion held so much power. At the same time, I feared the possible negative impact that much mana could have on the body. Mana was a useful thing, but an abundance of it could be terrifying. It could also do terrible things, like twist animals into monsters and transport children from the Central Continent to the Demon Continent. Although in this case, not being attacked by monsters did make our journey easier.

There were fixed intervals along the highway where you could make camp. It was there that we spent our nights. Ruijerd would hunt down something in the forest for dinner, so we had no shortage of food. Occasionally beastfolk from a nearby settlement would come to sell their goods, but we had no need for additional food supplies.

There was also a great abundance of plants, as expected of a forest. Flowers that could be used as spices grew aplenty on the roadside. I used what I learned from the Plant Encyclopedia I read when I was a kid, and gathered some ingredients to season our food. I wasn't a very skilled cook, but I'd improved somewhat in the past year, albeit only going as far from terrible to less awful.

The Great Forest provided much higher quality ingredients than the Demon Continent did. Not just in terms of beasts, but normal animals as well. The rabbits and boars tasted delicious enough roasted without seasonings, but that wasn't good enough for me. Since we had the ingredients readily available, I wanted to eat more scrumptious dishes. I was greedy as ever in my quest for good food.

That was where Geese came in. Just as he'd professed, he was a master at cooking outdoors. It was like sorcery the way he took the nuts and wild grass I collected and turned them into seasoning, injecting the most delectable flavors into our food.

"I told ya. I can do anything!"

It wasn't empty boasting, either. The meat really was delicious.

"Amazing; hold me!" I threw my arms around him without thinking it through. Geese was disgusted by it. I was disgusted by it. Our feelings were mutual.

"I'm bored," Eris muttered as we were preparing our daily meal as usual.

Ingredient Collector: Ruijerd

Fire and Water Producer: Me

Cook: Geese

Our job assignment was so on point that there was nothing for Eris to do except collect firewood, but she finished that quickly enough. As such, she was bored.

At first Eris would just silently train with her sword. After being forced into repetitive drills by Ghislaine and myself, she could go on swinging her sword for hours. That didn't mean she found it fun, though.

Currently Ruijerd was out hunting, Geese was boiling soup, and I'd settled down to continue working on my figurine. This 1/10th-sized Ruijerd figure was taking quite a bit of time to complete, but I was sure I could sell it. I'd add options to it to increase its value as well. Using this figure, I would show people that the Superd were not to be attacked and instead could be befriended.

That aside, Eris was finding her boredom unmanageable.

"Hey, Geese!"

"What's wrong, Miss? Food's not ready yet." He took a test sip of the soup before glancing back at her.

Eris was standing in her usual pose, arms crossed and legs spread apart. "Teach me how to cook!"

"I'll pass." His reply was instant. Geese returned to cooking as if their conversation had never happened.

Eris looked dumbfounded for a moment, but she recovered quickly and yelled, "Why not?!"

"'Cause I don't want to."

"So, why not?!"

Geese let out a big sigh. "Okay, Miss. All a swords-person needs to think about is fighting. Cooking is a waste of time. All you gotta do is eat."

This was a man whose culinary skills went beyond his "just eat" mentality. He could open his own restaurant. He wasn't so good that it would make a certain gourmet king's jaw drop and have a beam of light shooting out of his mouth, but he was at least good enough that his restaurant would be moderately popular in its neighborhood.

"But, if I could cook…um…well, you know, right?" She hesitated to explain, stealing glances in my direction.

What is it, Eris? What do you want to say? Heh heh, go ahead and say it, I inwardly goaded her.

"Nope, no clue." Geese was being cold to her. I wasn't sure why, but he was being unusually harsh. He wasn't that way toward Ruijerd or myself, but he always sounded detached when he interacted with Eris. "You're skilled at the sword, aren't you? You don't need to know how to cook."

"But—"

"Being able to fight is a wonderful thing, you know? If you want to live in this world, there's nothing more essential than that. Don't waste your talent."

Eris' face turned sullen, but she didn't try to punch Geese. There was something strangely persuasive about what he said.

"That's my official reason." Geese nodded to himself and stopped stirring the pot. He then began filling the stone bowls I'd made. "See, I decided I'd never teach someone to cook ever again."

Geese had been in a dungeon diving party before. It was a party of six, an unskilled bunch who, unlike Geese, had only one role they could fulfill. At the time Geese had a habit of complaining, "You guys seriously can't do anything else?" Their party was unconventional, but effective at getting things done.

However, one day, a woman in the party approached Geese and said she wanted to learn how to cook. She wanted to go after one of the men in the party. Clearly the saying "the way to a man's heart is through his stomach" existed in this world, too. Geese responded with "Sure, I guess, why not?" and began teaching her.

It was unclear if the cooking had anything to do with what happened after, but the woman did get with the man and the two later married. Then they left the party and went off somewhere. That was fine, said Geese. There was a quarrel when the two left, but them leaving wasn't a problem.

It was what happened afterward that was horrible. When the two most important people left, the party fell to pieces. It became a maelstrom of squabbles and apathy, so much so that they couldn't undertake missions anymore and soon disbanded entirely.

Geese, however, was a man who could do anything. He had no talent for the sword or magic, but he could do everything else. That's why he thought he'd find a new party immediately. But that endeavor turned out to be an overwhelming failure. At the time, he was a somewhat well-known adventurer, yet no party would pick him up.

Geese could do anything. Anything any other adventurer could do. That was the problem, in other words. Other people could also do the things he could. If a party was highly ranked, they would split those menial tasks among their own members.

That's when Geese realized that the party he was in before was the only place he belonged. He was only who he was because they were all so unskilled. After that, Geese prematurely ended his career as an adventurer. Now he lived by gambling.

"And that's why I refuse to teach women how to cook."

Yet another jinx to add to his name. Although if you asked me, Geese's "jinxes" were a load of garbage. I saw no problem with him teaching her how to cook. This soup was delicious. One sip and jazz music started playing in your mouth. It was good enough that I wanted him to teach me too, so I jumped in to help.

"I understand you had something terrible happen to you, newbie, but that woman you helped found her happiness, didn't she?" I asked, with the added nuance of *So why don't you go ahead and teach Eris?*

Geese shook his head. "I don't know if she did or not. Never saw her after that." Then he let out a self-deprecating laugh. "But the man did not turn out happy."

Perhaps that was the reason for the jinx, then. I couldn't say anything after that, not after seeing the depressed look on Geese's face. The soup, which should have been delicious, suddenly didn't taste so great anymore.

I wondered just how much longer it would be before Ruijerd got back.

One day I found a curious stone monument on the roadside where we stopped to rest. It came up to my knees and had a strange pattern on its face. A single character was inscribed there, with seven motifs surrounding it. I was pretty sure the character was the word "seven" in

Fighting God tongue. As for the other patterns, I felt like I might have seen them before.

I decided to ask Geese. "Hey, newbie, what's this monument here?"

He looked and nodded in recognition. "That's the Seven Great Powers."

"The Seven Great Powers?" I echoed.

"It refers to the strongest people in this world—seven warriors."

The story went that when the second Great Human-Demon War ended, a person known as the Technique God came up with that name. At the time, the Technique God was considered to be one of the strongest people in the world. They selected seven people (themself included) and declared those people to be the strongest in the world. This monument was a way to immortalize who those people were.

"I believe Master Ruijerd knows more about it. Master Ruijerd!"

Geese called out and Ruijerd, who had been training nearby with Eris, came over. Eris fell back onto the ground with her legs and arms spread wide, trying to steady her breathing.

"'The Seven Great Powers', huh? Brings back memories." His eyes narrowed as he examined the monument.

"So you know about this?" I asked.

"I trained hard when I was young so one day one of the 'Seven Great Powers' would take me as a student." Ruijerd looked off into the distance as he spoke. Very, very far off... Wait, just how far back into the past was he looking, anyway?

"What's that pattern?"

"These are the motifs for each individual. They're pointing out the current seven names." Ruijerd motioned to each one and told me their names.

The current seven were (in order of hierarchy):

Number One - Technique God

Number Two - Dragon God

Number Three - Fighting God

Number Four - Demon God

Number Five - Death God

Number Six - Sword God

Number Seven - North God

"Hmm. But I've never even heard of the Seven Great Powers before." I said.

"The title was well known until Laplace's War."

"Why has it fallen out of use?"

Ruijerd explained. "Laplace's War brought about great change. Half of those listed went missing."

Apparently, with the exception of the Technique God,

the Seven Great Powers had all participated in Laplace's War. Among them, three were killed, one went missing, and another was sealed away. The only one who made it out in one piece at that time was the Dragon God. After several hundred years, with those at the bottom swapping spots for the strongest, the phrase fell out of use. Currently, the whereabouts of the four at the top were unknown.

TECHNIQUE GOD: Missing
DRAGON GOD: Missing
FIGHTING GOD: Missing
DEMON GOD: Sealed Away

It wasn't much of a ranking system when those confirmed to be the strongest were absent. That was why the title 'Seven Great Powers' fell out of use and faded from people's memories...or so it seemed. Incidentally, the reason the Demon God hadn't been removed from this ranking because he wasn't dead; he'd merely been sealed away.

"I wonder how many people from that time period are still alive?"

"Who knows," Ruijerd said. "Even four hundred years ago, people doubted whether the Technique God even really existed at all."

"Why did the Technique God create this list in the first place?" I asked.

"Hard to say. It was said they created it so they could find people capable of defeating them, but I don't know."

Almost like the Fukamichi Rankings.

"Well, this monument is pretty old, so maybe the actual rankings have changed anyway," I muttered.

Geese shook his head. "I heard that monument changes by itself through magic."

"Huh? Really, it does? What kind of magic?"

"As if I'd know."

So apparently the monument updated the ranking display on its own. I wondered how it did it. There was still so much magic in this world that I was unfamiliar with. I wondered if I would learn more about those types of magic by going to the University.

That aside, the Seven Great Powers, huh? Here I thought the world already had enough ridiculously strong people. It looked like I really couldn't keep up with the best of them. Not that I was aiming to be one of the strongest in the world, in particular. In fact, I decided it was best I didn't preoccupy myself with thoughts of that.

It took us a month to make our way out of the Great Forest. But that was it—just one month and we were out.

It was a completely straight road without a single monster. That's why we were able to devote our time entirely to travel.

That was one reason, at least. The other was because our horses were highly efficient. The horses of this world had an insane amount of stamina. They could run for ten hours in one day without rest, then nonchalantly do it again the next day. Perhaps they were using some kind of magic, but either way we made it smoothly out of the forest.

As for accidents, the only one we had during our journey was me getting hemorrhoids. Of course I didn't tell anyone, and secretly cured them with healing magic.

Eris spent her time standing on top of the carriage, claiming that it was part of her training. I told her to stop because it was dangerous, but she only huffed back that it wasn't, it was for balance training. I tried to do the same, but my legs and hips were trembling in agony the next day. It gave me a new respect for Eris.

Just past the Blue Wyrm Mountains, there was a rest station nestled in a small city at the entrance to a valley. It was run by dwarves. There was no Adventurers' Guild. It was famously known as a smithing city with weaponsmiths and armorers lined up side-by-side.

Geese told me the swords sold here were cheap and of good quality. Eris looked wistful, but we didn't have the extra money to spend on anything. Besides, it would no doubt cost a pretty penny to take a Superd with us from Millis to the Central Continent. I persuaded Eris against buying something on the grounds that we couldn't afford unnecessary spending. The sword she was using right now wasn't bad, anyway.

Still, I was a man. It didn't matter how old I was internally, seeing sturdy swords and armor lined up like that still made my heart race, though my age (and appearance) did seem to matter to a salesclerk who laughed me off, saying, "I don't think these would suit you, kid." He was surprised to learn afterward that I was actually intermediate rank in the Sword God Style. Well, we didn't have the money anyway, so I was really just browsing.

According to Geese, this was where the road diverged. If you took the mountain path to the east, you would find a large dwarf town. To the northeast were the elves, and to the northwest was the vast land the hobbits inhabited. Perhaps the lack of an Adventurers' Guild in this town was an issue of location.

Also, apparently if you entered the mountains there was a hot spring. A hot spring! Now that was something that caught my interest.

"What the heck is a 'hot spring'?" Eris demanded.

"Hot water comes rising out of the mountain," I explained. "It feels really good to bathe in."

"Yeah? That sounds interesting. But Rudeus, isn't it your first time coming here? Why do you know that?"

"I-I read it in a book."

Was that written in the *Wandering the World* guidebook? I somehow felt like it wasn't. Still, a hot spring. That sounded nice. Though surely this world didn't have yukata. Still, imagining Eris with her wet hair and her peachy skin, spacing out as she submerged herself in the warm water...

No, it probably wasn't a mixed facility anyway. I mean, right? But on the off chance it *was* a mixed facility, then how amazing would that be? Now I really did want to check it out.

As I was busy debating the issue in my head, Geese made his opposition known. "The rainy season just ended, so it's a mess right now in the mountains." It would take too much time for us to make our way up there since we were unused to traversing the mountains.

And so, I gave up going to the hot spring. What a bummer.

The Holy Sword Highway was stretched across the Blue Wyrm mountains. Its path cleaved the mountain range in two, creating a space just wide enough for two horse-pulled carriages to make their way past one another. It was a ravine, but thanks to the divine protection of Saint Millis, rocks rarely came falling from above. If this path didn't exist, we would've had to take a more indirect path by traveling north.

Although blue dragons were a rare encounter in the mountains, there were still many monsters. Trying to pass through the range presented a considerable danger. Instead, Millis had created a shortcut straight through where monsters wouldn't appear. I could see why this saint had been so highly praised.

We made it through the valley in three days, completing our long, arduous journey out of the Great Forest. Straight from there was the Holy Country of Millis. We had finally returned to the domain of men, a fact which made my heart leap as I continued my journey.

Guardian Fitz

B Y THE TIME he realized what was happening, he was in mid-air.

"Huh?!"

The wind instantly swallowed his cry of disbelief.

He was incredibly high up. He could feel himself falling quickly. The force of the wind made it difficult to breathe. He was piercing the clouds, and fear was piercing him.

"Eek!"

He could hear it, a cry from deep in his throat. It was his cry, but it sounded so distant that it felt like someone else screaming. The cry reassured him that this was reality. He didn't know why, but he was in the air and he was falling.

"Ah...ah!"

He had to do something. He had to do something or he was going to die. Yes, die. There was no doubt he would die. If you fell from a high enough place, you died. He knew that. He also knew that the ground was rapidly approaching.

"Waaaaaah!"

He succumbed to the fear and unleashed all of his mana. It was wind. He was unleashing wind. It felt as though it were striking him from directly below. Who was it that taught him that a bird rides the wind to fly in the sky? He couldn't remember.

The speed of his fall slowed momentarily, then quickly returned to its previous pace. Wind magic wasn't going to cut it. Birds may have ridden wind to fly in the sky, but no matter how much wind you put under humans, they could not fly. Someone taught him that. Who? He couldn't remember that, either.

What was he supposed to do in a situation like this? His teacher had told him something. His teacher taught him a lot of things. What was it that his teacher had said?

Think, think, he chanted to himself.

His teacher said something about…how to fly? That's right, about how it was impossible. You couldn't fly—humans couldn't fly. You had to use something in order to fly. His teacher had tried to fly before. Tried, failed, and put something on the ground, something soft to fall on.

That was it! Something to soften the fall. Something soft. Something soft to wrap around himself. But just how soft was it supposed to be? How was he supposed to make it?

I don't know, I don't know, I don't know! he screamed in his head. *What do I do, what do I do, what do I do?!*

He conjured water and tried to wrap it around himself. It didn't work. It scattered immediately. He conjured wind and tried to boost himself again. It failed. That wasn't going to work. He conjured earth...but he wasn't sure how to use it! He conjured fire and...the wind...water? Earth? He didn't know! He just didn't know anymore!

"Aaah!"

He fell headfirst.

"Waaaah!" A silver-haired boy screamed as he jerked his body upright and out of bed. He was somewhere around the age of ten, and his youthful features were contorted in fear.

"Hah, hah, hah..." He gasped for breath and began patting his body. His hands grabbed at fistfuls of silver hair, hard enough to tear them out. He was checking to see if his body was still in one piece.

"...Ah? Huh?" When he looked around, he realized he wasn't in the sky anymore. He was in a soft bed. "Hah..." The young boy covered his face with his hands and breathed a sigh of relief.

"Hey, Fitz, you okay?" A voice called out to him from above. Another boy was hanging upside down, peering at Fitz from the bed above. This other boy was at the cusp of adulthood. He was handsome enough to captivate any person who looked upon him, or so he claimed. His name was Luke. "You were making a lot of noise while you were sleeping. Did you have that dream again?"

"Oh, yeah..." The boy, known as Fitz, nodded vaguely in response. All of a sudden he realized his crotch area felt strange. Curious, he looked down to find it was damp. When he investigated, he found he'd drenched not only the bottom of his sleepwear, but the sheets beneath him as well. He could see the steam rising from them.

"Ah...!" Flustered, Fitz tried to pull up the covers to hide the mess from Luke, but it was already too late. Luke took in the sight of Fitz's accident with a frown on his face.

"Wah...waah..." Fitz looked pitiful, tears in his eyes, as he glanced at Luke. "I-I'm so...sorry..."

"Don't apologize to me." Luke climbed down from his bed and gave a sigh as he scratched at his head. "No one's going to blame you."

"B-but, I'm old enough by now…and yet I'm still…still, well, wetting myself like this…"

"You're not the only one who had a terrifying experience that day." Luke shrugged as he said it, but he had a serious look on his face. His tone was entirely sincere. "Besides, there's lots of guys here who soil their sheets at night. The maids are used to it. Now hurry up, get changed and hand your shirts over to the person in charge of washing. Lady Ariel is waiting for us." Once Luke finished speaking, he left the room.

Fitz wiped away his tears and crawled out of bed, grabbing his sunglasses from the nearby table and sliding them onto his face.

Fitz was a victim of the incident that decimated the Fittoa Region. He was transported into mid-air, a hundred meters above the ground. Like anyone else, Fitz was no exception to the law of gravity, so he fell.

The only thing unusual about him was that he was a magician. Not just any magician, either. He may have been only ten, but he had an exceptional teacher and was at least intermediate-tier in every school of magic, advanced in several, and he could cast spells without chanting.

He struggled as he was in the air. Before he made it to the ground, he managed to slow the speed of his fall and miraculously only broke both legs when he landed (crashed was more like it). His mana was completely drained and he fell unconscious.

Fitz woke up to discover he'd lost everything. His hometown, his house, his family. He was still so young, and in an instant he'd become a vagabond. He had nowhere to go and no one to rely on, except for the woman whose eye he'd caught, Ariel Anemoi Asura. She saw the way Fitz freely wielded magic without any incantations, so she employed him. After that, Fitz began his life in the royal palace as the guardian of the second princess.

"Mmmmhh... Oh, Luke and Fitz, good morning."

His work as guardian began with rousing Ariel. He woke her at a specific time every morning. This would normally be a lady-in-waiting's job, but Ariel had faced so many assassination attempts since she was a child that the duty now fell instead to one of her guardians, either Luke or Fitz. Fitz was only entrusted with the duty once

Ariel knew that he was a resident from outside the palace and not involved with any of the nobles she counted as enemies.

"Good morning, Lady Ariel."

Waking up any later than the princess was enough to warrant a harsh punishment. Or at least it was supposed to, but Fitz had woken up after Ariel any number of times and was never disciplined.

"It's a nice morning, isn't it? Luke, what are the plans for today?" Ariel stretched her body and slipped out of bed, taking a seat at her makeup stand. Fitz stepped in behind her to wash her face and comb her hair.

"After breakfast you have a meeting with Lords Datian and Klein to talk about..." As Luke calmly laid out her itinerary, Fitz made quick and careful work of untangling her hair. "In the afternoon you'll have a meeting with Lord Pilemon, and then dinner will be..."

"'Lord Pilemon'? As if you don't know him. Luke, that's your father, isn't it?"

"I've been told to keep business and private matters separate."

Once Fitz finished setting her hair, Ariel rose out of her seat and lifted her arms shoulder-high. Fitz immediately set about undressing her. Normally changing the princess' clothes would be a job for one of her ladies-in-waiting, but this was another custom she'd been practicing since she was a child.

Fitz felt flustered as he peeled away the beautiful silks that were wrapped around Ariel's vibrant white skin, exchanging them for clothes that a lady-in-waiting had prepared in advance. The clothing was complex, with a bizarre structure that Fitz wasn't even sure how to wear. Yet he managed to slip it briskly onto her body.

He wasn't even sure how to dress people when he was first assigned the job. But he'd become quite skilled at it. Even a country bumpkin like Fitz could learn after being forced to do the same thing over and over again.

"Fitz...you messed up one of the buttons."

"Huh? Ah, yes, I'm sorry." Just then he'd gotten distracted, and the princess pointed out his mistake. Fitz hurried to try and fix it, but he wasn't sure which button he'd slipped up on. With clothing like this, if you messed up a single step of the process it made it impossible to figure out where to start with fixing it.

"What's wrong?" the princess asked. "If you don't hurry up and get me dressed, I might catch a cold."

"Y-yes, you're right, please hold on just a moment!"

"Or do you want to see my body?" Ariel teased.

"N-no!"

His face turned bright red with panic as he denied her accusation. Ariel sniggered. She liked how innocent he was, so much so that she frequently picked on him like this.

"I think you look beautiful." Luke was always the one who jumped in to help during such interactions. He smiled and pointed to the buttonhole Fitz was searching for.

"Oh my, Luke, does that mean you're falling for your master?" Ariel cooed. "If so, that's equivalent to blasphemy. You won't be able to escape punishment for that."

"How terrifying. What kind of punishment are we talking about?"

"The kind where I confiscate all of your snacks for today," she said.

"Oh my. Well, that is quite severe. But if that's what my master desires, then so be it."

As the two of them continued their interaction, Fitz finally finished with her clothing. Ariel took a twirl to confirm that there were no imperfections in her outfit, then nodded in satisfaction.

"Nice work. Now then, let's have our meal."

"Yes, milady!"

Luke tailed Ariel as she walked out. Fitz moved to follow, but abruptly stopped to get a glimpse of his reflection in the mirror of her makeup stand. It showed a young man with a somber look, sunglasses over his eyes. He lingered there and twisted a strand of short-cropped white hair around one of his fingers. It only lasted for a moment. He turned away and trailed after Ariel.

The nobles were quite judgmental about the young guardian Fitz after his abrupt appearance in the royal palace.

"But there are so many among the Magician's Guild who were born to more noble families..."

His family and background were complete mysteries. The only things people knew about him were his race and the color of his hair. From his manners and way of speaking, it was clear that he wasn't nobility. Despite that, Ariel had appointed him as her new guardian. She gave him quality guardian equipment and kept him at her side constantly. Such special treatment only inflamed the nobles' disapproval.

"Can't something be done about those sunglasses at the very least?"

"I concur. It's almost as if the boy doesn't even understand the concept of respect."

He was always wearing sunglasses. In the imperial court, hiding your face without purpose was considered impolite.

The nobles' words were misinformed, however. Ariel had received permission from the king himself for the sunglasses. In fact, the sunglasses were a magical item that could sense when Ariel was in trouble, no matter where the wearer was. The item was deemed necessary after her previous "incident," so the king permitted it.

"Thanks to those sunglasses, the maids in the imperial palace keep screeching in such high-pitched voices."

"Yes, I've heard how it 'brings them such happiness' just seeing Fitz and Luke walking together."

"Indeed, nothing seems to make them happier than seeing a womanizer like Luke stepping in so valiantly to look after the boy."

"They're corrupting the morals of the imperial court."

"Not that the court particularly had any."

Hahaha, the nobles laughed.

Fitz was always following Ariel around, and you could tell the boy was handsome beneath those sunglasses. So seeing him, Ariel, and Luke together encouraged many to dream up wild fantasies.

"I realize they're both boys, but there's something odd."

"Oh? What's odd?"

"Luke professes, without hesitation, that he loves women and hates men, yet he's being unusually kind toward that boy."

"Ahh, I see what you mean. That's true."

"Yes, but there's nothing 'odd' about it. I'm sure it just means that Luke has finally come to understand the beauty of men as well, no?"

"No doubt, ha ha!"

Homosexuality was not considered unusual to Asuran nobles. There were those with far stranger sexual preferences, so boys who fell in love with other beautiful boys did not warrant any surprise.

"But just where in the world did the princess find that boy?"

"Who's to say? But for Princess Ariel to offer such support makes me wonder. Perhaps he's the illegitimate child of some high-ranking nobleman."

"Oh, so you *do* have an idea about where he's from, then?"

"Indeed. Several years ago I went to visit my cousin in the Fittoa Region. That cousin had attended the birthday ceremony for Lord Sauros' ten-year-old granddaughter."

"Oh, Lord Sauros' granddaughter... You mean the Boreas' red-haired monkey princess?"

"Yes, the one with the reputation for going to school and beating up other children her age. The one who neglected her studies so much she couldn't even greet people properly. *That* monkey princess."

"And what does that have to do with this?"

"Yes, well, according to my cousin's story, that monkey princess had changed quite a bit. She greeted people politely, behaved in a ladylike manner, and danced magnificently."

"I'm sure the rumors have just been embellished. Perhaps it's just that the monkey princess didn't behave as a monkey for once?"

"No, this was different. According to my cousin, when he greeted the liege lord, Sauros bragged to him about it."

"About what?"

"That the one who'd taught his granddaughter was a boy two years younger than her."

"Oh...the age does fit."

"The lord praised him so highly that my cousin began to suspect and even asked, 'Is this boy related to you?'"

"Oh my."

"Of course the lord didn't say as much, but I heard he didn't strongly deny it, either."

"So that's the story. Could that impressive youth be the boy Ariel's claimed as her guardian?"

"It could be."

"So that's the reason why the boy has such etiquette despite being a commoner."

It was then that another noble suddenly thought aloud, "But is he truly that strong?"

According to Ariel, Fitz was agile enough to put the court's knights-in-training to shame. He was also well-versed in reading, writing, and arithmetic, and held more intimate knowledge of magic than even the teachers at the University of Magic possessed. Not to mentioned he could use advanced-tier magic without any incantations, at only ten years of age!

"It must be a load of nonsense."

"Yet after what Princess Ariel has been through, it's hard to believe she would keep someone who wasn't strong at her side."

"Hmm, why don't we just see for ourselves? Peel off that boy's mask and see him for who he truly is…"

"I wouldn't advise that. If he really is that powerful, you'll only be causing trouble for yourself."

"True. Nevertheless, since he is a guardian, I'd at least like him to learn some of the traditions of the court."

"Agreed. I've had enough of him being a vulgar country bumpkin."

That was how the nobles criticized Fitz, maliciously gossiping about him as they watched, without any intention to act on their hostilities. Fortunately, that was exactly what Ariel expected them to do.

"Then shall we have Lord Tink's son enter the Knights' Guild?"

"Yes, he is skilled at arithmetic. Have him enter the guild and learn firsthand from the guild's accountant."

It was early afternoon. Ariel was meeting with Luke's father, Pilemon Notos Greyrat. Pilemon topped the list of Ariel's supporters. While he had poor judgment, he was a young man acting as the Liege Lord of the Milbotts Region. Every time something came up, he would pay her a visit to discuss the future.

Ariel currently didn't have many supporters. She wasn't an adult yet, and although she was popular with the general public, she didn't enjoy the same level of acclaim amongst the nobles. That was why they were presently laying groundwork with them.

The powerful, high-ranking nobles who backed the first or second prince wouldn't simply double-cross them to support Ariel. They had already established their positions within their factions.

That was why Pilemon suggested capturing the

undecided voters. This meant winning over noblemen from the countryside who didn't involve themselves with the continent's political disputes, as well as middle- and lower-ranking nobles who didn't hold much power. Then Pilemon would use his power to appoint them as government officials, placing those who were exceptional in lower (albeit important) positions.

Theirs was a strategy for the future, for ten or twenty years from now. A decade from now, those who supported Ariel thanks to Pilemon's work would be in various key positions (even if they weren't at the top) and would provide great support for her.

"The Knights' Guild, the Magicians' Guild, the Imperial Guard, and the City Watch... For these, we've laid the groundwork for all the key positions."

"It's too early to say if the seeds we planted will bear fruit. It's possible someone will see through our plan and pull it out by the root."

First, they worked to suppress the military's strength and make it their own. In this era of peace, soldiers and knights weren't valued as highly as before. Their work consisted of eliminating monsters and thieves, at most. One could say they had no political power, which was why the other factions didn't try to get their support.

Still, if something were to happen, the military would be the one to take action.

The Asura Kingdom hadn't seen a civil war in a long time. As long as there was no solid proof left behind, even assassination in the court was permissible. Consequently, the nobles had forgotten the power of the military. Ariel and Pilemon, on the other hand, worked first and foremost to obtain the military's support.

"It's vexing to have to take such roundabout measures like this."

"Indeed." Pilemon was the head of the Notos Greyrat family, but he was younger than the other Greyrats and didn't have much in the way of popularity or coin.

Ariel was similar. She was part of the royal family, so she could use money freely, but it was clear at a glance that a huge gap lay between her and the other candidates. Her only edge was her popularity with the people, and popularity was quick to fade. The other princes didn't do much to change the peoples' hearts. Popularity was too fickle to use as a linchpin.

But just who was it that she was fighting, and for what purpose?

"But Your Highness, a solid and steady path is the quickest one."

"Yes, of course. I know that. Obtaining the crown requires one to take the winding road."

It was because Ariel had resolved to become the queen. She had begun down the path that would lead her to the throne.

While those in the court had their attention focused on Fitz, Ariel worked in the background to strengthen her ties with those influential nobles that supported her, quietly waging a political war of her own.

She donned the mantle of the terrified princess, frantically trying to protect herself. It was like an invisibility cloak that hid her lion's teeth as she moved forward. Just as her deceased former guardian Derek Redbat had wished of her.

"..."

Two people stood guard as Pilemon and Ariel worked on personnel affairs. Luke and Fitz watched quietly, not involving themselves in the conversation.

If a merchant or adventurer with a keen eye were to see the equipment the two wore, they would gasp in surprise. Both were completely decked out in magical items. Fitz and Luke each wore Boots of Swiftness that allowed them to run at twice the normal speed, a Flame Trapping Cloak that kept them at a constant body temperature without letting heat pass through it, and Gloves of Overpowering that reduced any impact to the palm of the wearer's hand by half. In addition, at Luke's waist was a Steel-Cutting Sword that could easily tear straight through a steel shield.

From weapons to armor, the equipment was perfect. Ariel had obtained them all after her previous incident. Only the wand that Fitz held was different. It was a small rod, the exact sort given to an apprentice who was just beginning to learn magic. This was neither a magic item nor a magical implement.

"Well then, Lord Pilemon, thank you for your time."

"Yes. And Princess Ariel, this could be the perfect opening for someone to discover what we are planning, so be sure not leave any gaps for them."

"Indeed."

As Luke and Fitz guarded them, Ariel and Pilemon concluded their meeting. They both looked satisfied as they cut across the room and headed for the door. In response, Luke matched Ariel's pace and fell in line directly behind her. Fitz was slightly slower, but followed Luke's example.

"Luke, make sure you protect her ladyship."

"Ha ha."

Pilemon left his son with that message before he took his leave. As he watched his father go, Luke bowed as custom demanded.

"Phew...that took quite a bit of time. Let's eat, shall we?"

"Yes, Princess." Luke rang the bell to summon the servants. It chimed three times. When a lady-in-waiting appeared, he instructed her to prepare the food and then returned to his spot behind Ariel.

Fitz watched the entire interaction with great interest. "Is there some kind of a system with that bell? As in, do you ring a certain number of times to call for food?"

"Of course not. It's just a normal bell," Luke said with exasperation.

Fitz pushed his lips out in a pout and nodded. "Ah, okay. I guess that makes sense."

Lately Fitz asked Luke questions like that all the time, including ones about mealtime manners and greeting etiquette. Fitz himself had little more than vague knowledge of such things, which was why other nobles would laugh at his expense at every turn. Each time, he would flush with embarrassment and then ask Luke the proper etiquette so that he could nail it perfectly next time.

"Hee hee." Ariel giggled at their conversation. "Fitz, you've finally started getting used to court etiquette lately, haven't you?"

"Not at all. I have a long way to go."

"Seeing how hard you're working would warm anyone's heart."

"I'm not so sure. The other nobles seem to hate me, at least." Fitz pursed his lips in another pout and turned to look at Luke. The latter just looked away as if the matter had nothing to do with him.

"The gossip of the rabble is nothing to concern yourself with. I like you," the princess said.

"...Thank you." Fitz didn't look particularly happy about it, but he bowed his head to Ariel. "On another note, Princess, have you found my family or my master yet?"

Ariel shook her head weakly. "No..."

Fitz had agreed to become Ariel's guardian with a few conditions of his own. The first of which was that she would forgive his crime of entering the palace without authorization. Fitz had appeared suddenly on the day of the Displacement Incident. Even though it wasn't of his own volition, he had entered the grounds without permission, which was a punishable offense according to the Asura Kingdom's laws. At Ariel's discretion, he was spared discipline, though that would surely have happened regardless, given that he did save her life in the process.

The other condition was that she search for the friends and family from whom he'd been separated. Given that the incident occurred in the Fittoa Region, the liege lord of that region (Boreas) should have overseen this duty.

But the Boreas family had lost all their land and the people under their command along with it.

Those nobles who considered the Boreas family their enemies saw a perfect opportunity and eagerly launched their attack. It was all the family could do to try to preserve their position. They didn't have the luxury of searching for missing residents. They had organized something resembling a search party, more or less, but it was little more than for show. So Ariel used her pocket money to assemble a team and commanded them to search.

Incidentally, the high-ranking minister Darius, who supported the first prince, would later take the Boreas family under his protection and invest in a search party. A search party that would swell in size, but... Well, that's a story for another time.

With those two conditions attached, Fitz became Ariel's guardian and protector.

"I don't know the whereabouts of your family. As you know, they have been scattered throughout the world."

"Yes...I understand." Fitz's face fell, enough that anyone who saw would feel pity for him.

Ariel noticed and had a rare look of distress on her face. "Fitz...I apologize. Right now I don't hold much power."

"No, I wouldn't have been able to do anything by myself, so I'm grateful for what you've done."

Ariel's expression turned pensive as she saw how bravely Fitz responded. Then she suddenly clapped her hands. "That's right! Fitz, come to my bedroom tonight."

"Huh?!" Her sudden proposal elicited an uncharacteristically loud squeak from Fitz.

"I heard that you've been having bad dreams lately, making a lot of noise in your sleep. If you sleep next to someone, that might alleviate the problem a bit, no?"

"B-but I'm just your bodyguard, a country bumpkin, and you're a princess... Luke, please say something!"

As the conversation suddenly turned to Luke, he flashed a prim and proper smile and said, "Why not accept her offer? Just think of it as a reward."

"A reward...?"

"Well, I'm sure it will stir some strange rumors, but you should be fine. You've endured their gossip thus far after all, right?"

Fitz had no allies here. Once he realized that, he heaved a sigh.

As Ariel and Pilemon were conspiring with one another, somewhere else in the imperial palace, another conspiracy was taking shape.

"How do Ariel's recent movements look?"

Two men conversed in a room. One was a young man with soft blond hair, somewhere in his mid-twenties. In one hand he held a wine cup made of Begaritt glass, which contained fresh wine from the Milbotts Region.

The other man was a portly fellow who looked to be in his early fifties. A half-naked girl was seated on his lap, and his hand was stretched toward her bottom. "A bit suspicious, I'd say." His voice was cold and his eyes burned with lust as he watched the girl. She blushed and looked down as he rubbed her butt.

The younger man didn't seem to mind. He just enjoyed the taste of his wine, churning the liquid inside his glass. "That doesn't tell me anything."

"I've gotten reports that she's inserted her own men into the Knights' Guild and the Imperial Guard."

"The Knights' Guild and the Imperial Guard? Damn that Ariel. Does she intend to perform a coup d'état?"

The older man slipped his hand into the girl's panties and shook his head. "Impossible. She's not that impatient. I'm sure she merely intends to increase her allies."

"But the Knights' Guild and the Imperial Guard don't hold any political influence."

"Aye, indeed. But there are many common folks among the Knights' Guild and the Imperial Guard. Those are the people easiest for Princess Ariel to work with. I'm sure that's only the beginning of her plans."

"Hm..."

The older man continued, "Besides, it's not like she has her own private army."

The younger man started thinking. The Knights' Guild and the Imperial Guard had no political power. The Asura Kingdom undoubtedly had the greatest military strength of any nation, but half of their soldiers were common folk. Those at the top were nobles and followers of his, so replacing them wouldn't be easy.

Still, the guild and the guard would be the first to move if anything happened in the imperial capital. If the captains and commanding officers were all replaced with people who supported Ariel, then the soldiers and knights under their command would ally themselves with her as well, given that she was more popular. In that case, he couldn't rule out the possibility of a coup d'état.

"That was a bit of a blind spot for me. It seems my younger sister is quite intelligent." There was admiration in his voice as he spoke.

The fat man just snorted in laughter as he played with the girl's body. "That's absurd. It's just a desperate act, I'm sure." A smile curved his lips as the girl's hushed moans began to grow. "However, desperate as it may be, it's a good move. I thought that neophyte Notos lad to be nothing more than an underhanded rat, but it seems he has some foresight after all."

"What should we do?" the younger man asked.

The fat man removed his hand from the girl's body. He dipped his fingertip in a glass of wine and jammed his finger, dripping with purple liquid, into her mouth. The girl didn't try to stop him, but merely licked at it. "There's nothing to be done," he said. "I've watched them quietly this past year. If they're going to be Your Majesty's enemies, Prince Grabel, then naturally we must dispose of them."

"By what means?"

The fat man brought his finger, which the young girl had been licking, to his lips and swirled his tongue around it. "Instead of plucking the buds, let's get rid of the one sowing the seeds."

"All right, Darius. I leave it to you."

"As you command, my prince."

The First Prince Grabel and the high-ranking Minister Darius resembled a couple of corrupt Edo period officials as they conspired in the seclusion of a private room. The only person who overheard their talk was the female slave resting atop Darius' lap. And that girl just happened to be...

It was late at night, a time for everyone to be resting in their beds, when Fitz arrived in Ariel's chambers. Steam was visibly rising from his face.

"Um, Princess Ariel, I'm here like you asked."

Before he came, Ariel's ladies-in-waiting had taken him to the bath, smeared his body in scented oils, and changed him into high-quality nightwear woven from soft fabric.

"Glad you came. You can leave now," she said to her two ladies-in-waiting. They each bowed before slipping out of the door. Fitz and Ariel were suddenly alone together in her dimly lit room. "What's wrong? Come over here and take a seat beside me."

"O-okay." Fitz did as he was told, nervously sinking down beside the princess.

Ariel moved her body closer to his.

Fitz moved his body farther away. Then, slightly panicked, lifted his hand to stay her. "Uh, um...we're just sleeping together, right?"

"Yes, of course."

"Um...uh...you say that, but you have a scary look in your eyes."

Ariel gradually sidled closer, and Fitz hurriedly put more distance between them.

"There's nothing scary about this. It's true, I do feel

excited by the glossy look of your skin, but it's all right. I won't do anything. Now, lie down on the bed."

"No, it's scary. You're scaring me, Princess!"

"There's nothing to be afraid of," Ariel cooed back.

"No, I'm saying... I'm, you know. You do know, right? That I'm actually—"

"I know," she said. "Of course I know."

At last she'd cornered Fitz on the very edge of the bed. Ariel put her hand on his shoulder and forced him against the mattress. "That's why I would like you to learn more about me as well."

Fitz snapped his eyes shut as if he were a virgin. It was too much for him, so he acquiesced, entrusting his body to her hand. After all, Fitz had no relatives to turn to, so he couldn't go against Ariel's wishes.

"That was a joke. I'll stop here," the princess said. She lifted herself away from him and plopped down beside him instead, lying on her back.

Surprised by this, Fitz turned his head and their eyes met. "Um..."

"I told you, didn't I? That we're just going to sleep together. Are you getting the wrong idea? You thought I would force myself on you?"

Fitz went bright red all the way to his ears. Ariel laughed when she saw it. "True, seeing the face you're making right now makes me want to do it, but today I really am just going to sleep beside you." She looked up and exhaled.

Fitz remained confused, unsure of what he should do. His body turned rigid.

For a while silence fell between them. The one who finally broke it was Ariel. "Me too," she said. "I've been dreaming, too."

"Dreaming?"

"Yes, about that day. About Derek being killed by that monster, and it turning on me to devour me next. That nightmare." Fitz looked at Ariel's face again. Her usual gentle smile was gone, leaving a blank, transparent expression. "I have that dream all the time. I struggle in my sleep and finally jolt awake once it's over. It's gone on for days now."

"For you too?" Fitz asked.

"Yes." Ariel nodded and squeezed his hand in hers. Her fingers were dainty and thin, so much so that they seemed like they could break at any moment. Yet the strength of her grip assured him that she was full of life. "Fitz, I can't understand your pain, but you weren't the only one who experienced pain that day. If you're having a hard time, you can lean on someone."

"Thank you…"

"That's why I didn't hesitate to lean on you. Perhaps if I sleep beside the person who saved me that day, then I won't have that nightmare anymore."

Those words were strangely relaxing to Fitz. It was as if she knew that he hadn't been able to relax since the Displacement Incident. She realized how he struggled to earn her approval, bluffing so she wouldn't think he was useless, working hard so she wouldn't dismiss him out of hand.

"I understand now..."

None of that was necessary. Ariel would surely have kept him at her side even if he couldn't use magic, because he was someone who could understand her pain.

"Princess Ariel?"

"What is it?"

"I'm going to do the best that I can as your guardian," he said.

"That's a good attitude to have. But for the time being, I hope you'll do so in my dreams." She chuckled.

As if encouraged by her laughter, Fitz felt a smile rise to his lips, too. It was his first since the incident one year ago.

"All right, then let's go to sleep."

"Yes, Princess. Good night."

Ariel kept her fingers around Fitz's hand as she closed her eyes.

Fitz also closed his eyes, anticipating the comfort of sleep. But then, just as he was about to let go of his consciousness, he realized something.

"Huh...?"

There was a presence in the room. Just a few moments ago the only ones he'd sensed were his own and Ariel's, but there was someone standing by the bed. A young girl. She was hovering by their bedside in scanty clothing that barely hid her nether regions, and in her hand she carried a large knife.

The girl moved the moment Fitz's eyes met hers. She threw herself at Ariel in an attempt to attack.

Fitz realized she was an assassin, but before he could scream anything, his body was already moving. In the same instant that he leaped to shield the princess' body, he held out both hands toward the girl and released his magic. "Air Burst!"

"Gah!" The magic, which had been cast without any incantations, hit the girl directly, throwing her away from where Ariel was laying.

"What's going on?!" the princess cried out.

"Princess! It's an assassin! Please get behind me! Luke, it's an enemy attack!" Fitz's voice echoed. The guardians' room was right beside the princess', so Luke should come quickly.

"Phew..."

The assassin stood up. Her eyes turned to Fitz and Ariel, flitting between the two of them before finally fixating on Fitz. It seemed she planned to finish off the bodyguard before she dealt with her target.

Finding himself on the receiving end of the intruder's gaze, Fitz lowered himself into a battle-ready stance. He was still dressed in his bedclothes without a single piece of his extravagant equipment on him, but it did not diminish his fighting spirit.

"...Hssh!" The assassin dashed forward, heading straight toward Fitz.

Fitz turned both palms outwards and unleashed his magic. "Hah!" There was no form to the mana that flowed from his hands. The sound of an explosion was accompanied by the canopy bed being blown away, leaving a hole in the wall.

This was an advanced-tier spell, Sonic Boom. There weren't many who could face an explosion like that and live. Yet the assassin was still alive. She'd made it seem as though she were rushing toward him before she leapt to the side. A feint. Whether intentional or coincidental, the assassin had effectively evaded Fitz's attack. Then she whipped her knife through the air. It flew straight toward Ariel.

Fitz instantly stretched his hand out in the air as if to try to catch it. Of course, catching a knife flying through the air was no easy feat. Luckily it caught the tips of his fingers, slicing through his skin and disrupting its trajectory.

Having failed in her execution technique, the assassin switched to defense, almost like a cat trying to maintain its distance.

"Ah...!"

In seconds she was sent flying through the air by Fitz's second round of magic. The direct impact severed all four of the assassin's limbs, and she was left reeling through the air, falling out of the hole in the wall and into the dark of night.

"Hah...hah...."

The sudden switch from defense to offense left Fitz winded as he peered out the hole. It was a moonless night, so it was exceptionally dark out. He couldn't be sure what he saw below, but the assassin had taken that fall with her limbs severed. There was no way she was still alive.

"Phew..."

The feeling that he'd killed someone hadn't sunk in yet.

"Oh...Princess Ariel, are you all right?" He hurried back into the room to confirm she was safe. Midway there, his legs turned into noodles. "H-huh?" The tips of his toes went numb and he collapsed on the spot, his body giving out from beneath him.

Poison...! It was already too late by the time he realized, and his whole body began to shake as his consciousness grew dim. *Detoxification magic...!* If Fitz had been an ordinary magician, or if he hadn't been able to execute his spell without chanting, then he probably would have died instantly.

Even as his consciousness was consumed by darkness, he managed to cast the detoxification magic. Then he looked at his surroundings. Ariel was safe, and although he'd arrived late, Luke was there too.

"Luke, the assassin! Fitz defeated him, but he's been poisoned! Call the doctor immediately! And the Imperial Guard. I think the assassin's body fell down below."

"Understood!" Luke nodded and rushed down the stairs as he called for the guard.

Fitz watched, still feeling faint, and only lost consciousness once Luke was out of sight.

Thus, the attempted assassination of Ariel was over.

Fitz had been infected by the poison, but the cut on his finger was so small that only a little bit of it entered his system. Thanks to his quick response in using detox-ification magic, he narrowly escaped with his life and there were no lingering effects from the poison.

When he returned to the palace, the nobles' impressions of Fitz had changed. It was because of the assassin he'd defeated that day. Her remains had fallen into the courtyard, where the guard found them. She was identified as a famous assassin who had been working in the Asura Kingdom for the past ten years, known as the Night's Eye Crow.

A number of nobles had fallen victim to her blade before. The fact that Fitz had defeated her demonstrated that his strength was genuine. Since he used voiceless casting and didn't usually speak much, he was dubbed "Silent Fitz", and recognized by all the nobles as being worthy of his position as Ariel's guardian.

With that, the matter was resolved and peace prospered around Ariel...or so it appeared. No story ever closed its curtains so easily. From that day on, more assassins appeared to claim Ariel's life, one attack after another.

Each one of them was dispatched by Fitz's capable hands, but they never stopped and no culprit was ever identified. The Knights' Guild conducted their investigations, but someone was putting pressure on them, leaving the cases unsolved.

Ariel was mentally cornered and rendered exhausted by the fact that, although she could be relatively certain who was sending these assassins, she could not bring their identity to light. As a result, Pilemon determined that it was too risky for her to remain and proposed a plan for her to leave the country under the guise of studying abroad. But that is a story for another day.

Guardian Fitz had lost those closest to him in the Displacement Incident, disrupting his entire life. Though it wasn't of his own volition, he found himself being dragged deep into the Asura Kingdom's bloody political battle.

However, there was one good thing. After the day of Ariel's attempted assassination, he stopped having nightmares—the ones where he was sent flying through the air, futilely struggling until he smashed against the ground. That, at least, might have been his one mercy.

There is still some time yet in our story before the fates of this young man and Rudeus Greyrat intertwine.

ABOUT THE AUTHOR
Rifujin na Magonote

Resides in Gifu Prefecture. Loves fighting games and cream puffs. Inspired by other published works on the website *Let's Become Novelists*, they created the web novel *Mushoku Tensei*. They instantly gained the support of readers, and became number one on the site's combined popularity rankings within the first year of publishing.

"I don't mind if I fail in the process, as long as I get some experience," the author said with a grin.

Experience these great light **novel** titles from Seven Seas Entertainment

See the complete Seven Seas novel collection at
sevenseaslightnovel.com